HELL SPAWN

SAINT TOMMY, NYPD - BOOK 1

DECLAN FINN

HELL SPAWN

SAINT TOMMY, NYPD BOOK ONE

By Declan Finn

Published by Silver Empire: https://silverempire.org/

Cover design by Steve Beaulieu.

Dedicated to Albert E. Packard, good friend, and a great limbo dancer.

Chapter 1

ODD SAINT

My name is Detective Thomas Nolan, and I am a saint.

This is neither boasting nor an exaggeration.

I only had an inkling on the morning I chased Anthony Young, purse snatcher...again. Kid was your years older than my son. Young Anthony (see what I did there?), a 20th time offender, had upgraded to double duty, on this day both snatching the purse *as well as* the iPhone of Malinda Jones. Malinda was one of many careless New Yorkers who are so deep into their phones that they barely registered oncoming traffic, to heck with noticing a thief running up on them.

My radar was already up after Anthony bumped against me as he brushed past. I didn't bother checking for theft. I had nothing in the pockets of my tan overcoat, and my pants pockets were out of the reach of even a skilled thief. I merely continued my morning offering as the Opus Dei had taught me and was about to go into the Our Father.

Then Anthony charged forward, sweeping Malinda's purse from her shoulder, and plucking the iPhone from her hand. It was the latest model, over a thousand dollars' worth of technology in one easy-to-steal package.

Obviously, Anthony didn't see the all-caps NYPD emblazoned in gold letters on the front AND back of my policeman-blue baseball cap.

To make matters worse—for him—was that he did this in front of the mental health court for Queens, heralded by the black wrought-iron fence about ten feet high, which was serviced by the NYPD as their security. Further down the block was a housing community with its own private security.

In short, there was no real way that Anthony was going to get to the end of the (admittedly very long) block.

I was still under an obligation to chase the idiot. "Freeze! Police!" I barked before I took off after him. As expected, it made him run faster, but he obviously heard me, so he had his fair warning.

I pounded along the pavement behind Anthony, who was built for speed over anything else. He was short and slight, but he could run. I was bigger, a bit over six foot, and broad in the shoulders. Every big man will tell you one thing—running was just a great way to destroy your ankles and your knees if you do it right. I was a lumbering truck chasing after a motorcycle, but the moment Anthony ran out of gas, the impact would be similar.

As I ran, I mentally recited the Our Father and was on the Hail Mary when the strangeness happened. Suddenly, I could see myself ahead of Anthony... while at the same time, standing in front of him, I saw myself chase *behind* Anthony. It was a strange, vivid experience, with each view of Anthony as clear as the highest definition television—with almost more clarity than real life.

It was odd, but I was also too busy to ponder it. I held out an arm, leaned into it, and Anthony just ran into my arm. He clothes-lined himself so hard, his feet left the ground. I swept back under him as fast as I could, catching him just before his head hit the concrete. It wouldn't do for him to have brain damage over a stolen purse—it wasn't like he had little gray cells he could afford to lose.

I smiled into his face. "Hi Anthony. Would you like to tell me *your* rights? We've done this dance too often."

He merely smiled widely and shrugged, even as I hauled him to his feet. "Eh, you win some, you lose some. Still ain't gonna serve any jail time."

Anthony was a poster boy for juvenile recidivism and a great example for anyone who agitates for prosecuting all criminals as adults. He wasn't necessarily a bad kid, but he could use an extended stay in Boys Town—or an overnight in Rikers Island to scare him straight.

"It would help if you won *any*," I suggested.

"Can I cuff myself this time?" he asked as I took his wrists behind his back and cuffed them. "Guess not."

I rolled my eyes. "Anthony, have you considered that if you want money, you get a real job?"

He laughed. "You mean work for a living? Hey, that's racist, yo."

I shook my head and sighed. This kid was going to give me a headache. "Meet me halfway, find a crime you're at least good at?"

Malinda caught up to us at long last. She was 48, 4'9", and 180 pounds, so it took her a while. She looked at the perpetrator and frowned. "Anthony Young! I should have known. Just wait until I tell your gramma! Wait until I tell Father Pawson!"

Anthony finally looked concerned. "Aw, come on, Missus Jones, do you have to? I didn't know it was you."

Malinda wound up for a smack to the back of his head, and I twisted him around to put myself between them. "Mrs. Jones, you can't do that. I've got him cuffed already."

Malinda glowered. "Fine. But you take him right to the station. I'm going to meet you there. Taking my stuff. How dare you, Anthony!"

She stormed off ahead of us, not even waiting for me to hand her stuff back. I pocketed her phone and slung the purse over my shoulder—it was big enough to be a satchel, if worse came to worse.

"How'd you get in front of me, anyway?" he asked. "I don't remember you being that fast."

I blinked. That was a good question, to which I didn't have a good answer. I had heard that deja vu was simply a matter of slow communication between two halves of the brain. Perhaps it was serious brain lag?

No, that explanation didn't even work for me at the time, but since I didn't have a good answer for him, I merely told him the truth: "I haven't the foggiest notion."

"Ugh. Do you gotta use all the big words, Tommy?"

Argh.

As we walked down Winchester boulevard, we had a brief conversation in which Anthony read me his rights, and we confirmed that he wouldn't be getting a lawyer but a phone call to his mother.

Anthony was sulking by the time we got to 222nd street, and we passed in front of his public school on the way to my precinct. The school and the precinct were diagonally across the street from each other. An outside observer could tell that it wasn't a typical precinct, since the patch of grass to the right of our walkway had a full-color statue of Our Lady of Lourdes about two feet high, and the left had a statue of Jesus. Did our Catholicism show any? Just don't tell the ACLU.

This was the 105th precinct, otherwise known as the "French Bread" precinct. Since it was on the border of Queens and Nassau, Long Island, the boundaries of the Precinct followed the border. You could almost see that it was the last precinct established as the population went East—the 105 got whatever was left over. It went from Queens Village, Cambria Heights, Laurelton, Rosedale, Springfield Gardens, Bellerose, Glen Oaks, New Hyde Park, and Floral Park. If you're looking on a map, that means it stops at Rockaway Boulevard at the south end, Francis Lewis Boulevard at the west, and the Grand Central parkway to the North. Since the border on the East was uneven, so was our boundary. And, since the western boundary followed Francis Lewis, it came down at an angle. (Manhattan has the famous grid pattern layout to their streets. In Queens, they followed former cow paths that wandered all over the place.)

We entered the station, and I waved to the black woman at the front desk, Sgt. Mary Russell. She was 5'8", stocky, with short corn-rows that didn't travel too far down the neck. As far as fashionable hairstyles for women cops went, it was probably the closest equivalent to a crew cut.

"Hey, Tommy," she called. "You brought us a repeat customer, and you didn't even sign in yet? You bucking for another promotion?"

I nodded at her as I tugged on Anthony's cuffs, bringing him to a stop. "Mary, I found this wayward son on the way to the office this morning."

Sgt. Russell rolled her eyes. "I don't think community policing works like that."

I smiled. "It is when you live and work in the parish." I patted Anthony on the shoulder. "If you could call his mother? I think she's number nine in the speed dial by now. I—"

At that moment, I was hit by the *smell*. It was so repulsive that when it hit me, I gagged, and nearly vomited. It was horrific, and ungodly, and those were adjectives I used before I knew the source. If you've ever found a rotted human corpse, perhaps one dredged up from a body of water, you have an idea of what the stench was like. Then add in rotten eggs, fecal matter, sit and stew on a hot summer day for six hours.

This was worse.

I spun around for the nearest waste basket, expecting to vomit. I gathered myself together, and slowly composed myself, struggling to keep my breakfast down.

"Hey, Nolan, you okay?" Russell asked me.

I stayed there a moment longer, then straightened and turned back towards her. Even Anthony looked concerned.

Hand over my nose, I asked, "Don't you smell that? Smells like something died in the vents and cooked there."

Russell and Anthony shared a glance and a shrug. "Nope."

I took a slow, controlled breath, then scanned over the station. There wasn't anyone there who appeared that dank, dirty and unwashed. For someone to smell that bad, the only presumption was that he, she, or it looked like they had slept in garbage. But everyone there looked relatively tidy. Even one or two of the obvious drunks (red noses, half asleep, barely responsive to the officers with them) looked cleaner than I expected for such a repulsive odor.

I cautiously moved forward, taking small sniffs every few steps, just to keep tabs on the smell. Even that little was unbearable. Anthony stayed with Russell, and I worked my way through the station methodically. Whatever it was had to be toxic—and if only I could smell it, that didn't bode well in the long run for everyone else. If I were going insane, all well and good, but if it was real, things like a generally odorless, colorless gas, unleashed in a police station, could have all sorts of implications, and could end badly all around.

The source was what most civilians would picture as a "typical" junkie—the type who has obviously hit bottom, He was anemic, malnourished, scrawny, and painfully underweight. At 5'8, he may have weighed all of one hundred pounds. His hair was black, stringy, and greasy, and his eyes were a pale, watery blue. I couldn't tell if he was about to cry or bite someone's nose off ... or just curl up into a ball and die, since he looked close enough anyway. Sunken cheeks, protruding cheekbones, and he hurt to look at. His hands were cuffed behind his back, but the elbows were so bony, I was concerned he could stab someone with those alone. lol

And he smelled like death, decay, and made the stench of garbage trucks smell sweet in comparison.

"Okay, Hayes," one of the officers told him, "you're almost done. You can be in your cell in a bit."

As I approached Hayes, he started, his back becoming ramrod straight. He turned to look at me. His face went from being passive and wishy-washy to a mask of rage. He roared loud enough to hurt my ears and make the cops around him flinch.

With a loud *crack*, his arms shot forward. He'd dislocated his left thumb to get out of the cuffs. He grabbed the nearest policeman, hurling him across the room with maniacal strength. The cop slammed into a desk, then smashed through a window.

The cop behind him grabbed on, and the perp whirled, smacking him aside. He grabbed the cop's nightstick, and cut the leg out from under the officer.

Hayes whirled on me, bellowing, "Era uoy tahw wonk I!"

Then he lunged.

Chapter 2

ALL HELL BREAKS LOOSE

Despite looking half-starved and sickly, I wasn't going to let Hayes hit me with a nightstick. As he threw himself at me, I turned my right shoulder to him and launched myself into him, slamming his chest. I heard a loud *crack* as we connected, and it came from him, not me. Hayes swung, and his arm banged into my chest. My left arm came up and wrapped around the arm. My right elbow came up, digging into his chest, and slammed right into his jaw. The next step was to disarm him.

Hayes whirled around, hurling me across a desk. I hit the floor with a thud, and the desk crashed right next to me. He bounded over the desk, looking nothing so much as a great black raptor.

With one foot planted on the floor, I pushed my hips off the tiles and kicked out with my other leg, planting the sole of my shoe solidly into his chest. He was light enough that the impact pushed him back, and he landed on his feet. He wound up for another swing, but I kicked out again, this time hitting his knee. The leg went out from under him, and he tried to plant on the floor and swing again.

A fellow officer charged in, wrapping his body around Hayes' arm. Hayes pushed off the floor with his good leg, and then stood … on both legs.

I blinked and stared for a second. *How's he even upright?*

A second officer came in, bear hugging Hayes around the waist. With his free hand, Hayes grabbed the officer's hair and pulled back, prying his head back so they were face to face. Hayes head-butted him, then tossed him aside, sending both him and the first officer to the ground. He spun, driving his left fist into the first officer's gut, making him release the nightstick. Hayes raised the weapon high, ready to take his head off with it.

That's when I tagged in, sacking him from the side, slamming him up against a wall. I drove my right forearm into his face, and punched into the arm holding the stick. I hit again, and the nerves I struck caused his fingers to pop open.

I kicked the stick away before Hayes growled and shoved off the wall, driving both of us into the center of the bull pen. Hayes growled again, giving a full roar, like Godzilla. "Nalon, tnias, eid lliw uoy."

Glass cracked all over the station house. I looked around at all the windows and computer screens that were suddenly broken or breaking. *What the Hell is this guy on? Meth? PCP?*

Hayes charged again, and I knew I shouldn't take a direct hit from him if I could avoid it. I grabbed a chair, and used that to parry one of his windmill punches as I spun out of the way. I was a matador getting out of the way of the bull, and I used the chair to smack him on the back of the head as he passed. He went head-first into one of the windows, breaking the rest of it.

I didn't wait for his next move but followed after him, smashing the chair into his back. He was covered in glass and sparkling bits flung off of him as he spun around, knocking the chair from my grasp. I wrapped my right arm around him in a headlock, in order to hold him. My left arm wrapped under his right arm, so he couldn't bend in half and have a shot at striking my groin. My right side was essentially turned into him, so he couldn't knee me. He could stomp my instep or maybe grab my hair, but I expected both of those. While they could stun me, he wasn't going to get away.

That was when he thrashed like a wild thing and slammed me up against another window, breaking it and showering me with glass.

He kept spinning us around and growling. Apparently, Anthony Young had been placed at a desk while I had wandered off. The young man was cuffed to the desk and helpless as Hayes snapped at him with his teeth. Anthony leaned back as far as he could.

"Bad dog," I muttered. "Heel."

I wrestled Hayes back the other way, lifted him off the ground, and slammed him through another inside window.

Hayes kicked out, slipping out of my hold, jumping to the other side of the window, into an office. He turned around, probably thinking he could lunge back through,and gain momentum again. Unfortunately for him, I was already leaping after him and drove a foot into his face. He staggered back only a little and charged again. I sidestepped him, caught him by the shoulders, and hurled him out the office door. He effectively body-slammed a vending machine, crashing through the glass.

Hayes whirled around at me, his body a collection of cuts and his face a mask of blood.

And Hayes grinned like some demon released from a crimson-soaked Hell. "Em pots lliw gnihton. Tnias, em pots ton lliw siht."

"Sorry, I don't speak gibberish," I muttered. *Angels and ministers of grace defend us from the damned and the depraved.*

Hayes blinked, and the smile wavered.

With a little prayer, I burst forward, leading with a stopping elbow—slamming my entire forearm in his face. Hayes' head rocked backwards, and he came in swinging.

I leaned back, letting the fist go past my face, and my foot swung up, the front calf bone striking him full in the groin with the full force of my upper body. The blow lifted him off the ground, and his eyes widened in surprise, as though he were shocked that he felt pain.

My foot came down, and I leaned my body forward, my skull meeting his nose. He rocked under the force of the blow. I started a full running rosary through my mind as a way to keep my emotions in neutral. I grabbed him by his shirt, and spun him around, flat against the wall. I gave him a full body check against the wall, hoping to pin him there. I would have re-cuffed him, but if he was willing to dislocate one thumb, he wouldn't hesitate to do the other.

I muttered under my breath, "Holy Mary, Mother of God, prayer for us sinners, now and at the hour of our—"

Hayes screeched as though I had jabbed him with a hot poker. He writhed against the wall and struck it with his knee, pushing back at me just enough to get a hand on the wall. He shoved off, throwing me backwards and slamming me against a wall.

Someone ate his Wheaties this morning, I thought. *Forget PCP, what pharmacy is he on?*

Before Hayes could close with him again, he was swept away by six large, armored police officers, crashing into the maniac, and dog-piling him to the ground.

Hayes look at me with eyes filled with unchecked rage, and insanity. "Trapa it pir lliw I dna! Eid lliw evol uoy ginhtyreve! Eid lla lliw uoy! Tnias, eid lliw uoy!"

I looked to one of the officers and shrugged. I was as put off as he was and as confused. I smiled and covered with, "And I don't even know this guy. Imagine what it's like when they get to know me."

Hayes was taken away by all six officers, still screaming his gibberish, his feet off the ground. He thrashed and raged the entire way, kicking and struggling. One of his kicks knocked over another vending machine, leaving a hole in it as well.

I slumped against a wall and felt like taking a nap.

It then occurred to me that I hadn't even signed in yet.

This is going to be a heck of a day.

It was hours before everything was cleared up, statements were taken, desks were righted, glass was swept up, brushed out, and cleaned off of everyone. The station would be finding glass here, there and everywhere for months. Even I would be picking glass out of my pockets, and I needed a shower in the station locker room just to get the sharp bits out of my hair.

Speculation was rampant. On the job, we'd all seen things we couldn't explain before. Some of us ignored it, some of us became superstitious, and some of us just filed it away for later. Hayes had

been a radical new experience for everyone. He was the worst of
every meth head, combined with the worst legends of the bad old
days when PCP was a street drug—you know a drug is bad news
when even drug dealers stopped peddling it, lest their consumers go
into a frenzy and rip their heads off and use it for a basketball.
Among the suggestions were PCP, meth, and that Hayes had been
some sort of soprano who could shatter glass with a high note.

Two officers had discovered Hayes on a park bench where children played. They were going to simply roust him at first, before they
had discovered that he was using a bundle of bloody clothes as a
pillow, and his hands had been covered in blood that wasn't his.
There were also some dead animals littering the ground around
the bench.

In police work, we call this "suspicious."

The cuffs had been slapped on Hayes, and he barely did more
than giggle a few times. There was ID found on him, but he was
hardly responsive for the duration of his stay in police custody.

Then I showed up, and he became plenty responsive.

It was noon before anyone gave Hayes another thought. Two
police officers walked into the cells. They discovered Hayes hanging
from a light fixture in his cell, his pants having been made into a
makeshift noose.

Chapter 3

HEAVEN ONLY KNOWS

I f you ever wonder why there are cops who almost never seem to get the job done, I'll give you one possible explanation that doesn't include: "They're putting in the hours until they collect their pension." The short version? Paperwork. Dotting every i, crossing every T, eats up more time than is reasonable. It's why there are a lot of guys who don't bother with small arrests, like marijuana—if we arrested everyone who did it, we'd spend more time doing paperwork than anything else. Sad, but true.

This means that, even though I hadn't gone near Hayes before the confrontation in the station house that morning and I had been in plain sight of dozens of witnesses (and the cameras) since he was hauled away, my entire day had been eaten up by a skirmish that took less than five minutes. The cleanup, reports, filings, and all of that took until noon. Then Hayes was found dead. He was apparently dead a few minutes after he had been restrained in his cell.

It took an additional ninety minutes for two men from Internal Affairs to show up, Horowitz and McNally. They were both older men, which was unusual—the majority of IA guys liked getting the heck out of there when they can. It took a special sort of mindset to join the police only to hunt crooked cops. Some liked the power, and liked abusing it when they could get away with it. Some thought it was just something that needed to be done. Some enjoyed it.

In the case of Horowitz and McNally, they were casually known as Statler and Waldorf. Neither looked like the old heckling Muppets who critiqued *The Muppet Show*, but sometimes cop humor didn't necessarily have to hook onto anything but a superficial trait.

They broke out a tape recorder, placed it on the table, and hit record. They gave their names, my name, and the name of my PBA representative, who was also in the room. They added that this was part of the investigation into the death of Simon Hayes. It was the first time I had even heard his first name.

"Just to start with," McNally began, "we went over your file. You've never had any previous contact with the victim. Is that correct?"

"Not as a perp or as a victim," I answered. "Though I would be hard-pressed to call him a victim in this case. He did attack a room full of police officers, several of whom are in the hospital right now."

Horowitz nodded. "I noted your arrest history. It seems to be all over the place. You even seem to arrest people while you're not officially on the clock."

"I just want to do the job. I live in the precinct, and I do my duty. Is that a problem?

McNally shook his head. "No, not at all. But with your speed of promotion, we'd expected a little more emphasis on higher-profile crimes."

Horowitz caught the ping-pong ball of the conversation and threw it at me. "Looking at your arrest record, ever since you've been promoted to homicide, you still bring in the same criminals you were while you were in a blue-and-white."

"What can I say? I want to do the job at every level. Didn't think that was a crime."

McNally shrugged. "It isn't. But you're a little strange. You know that? People never complain about you."

I raised a brow. "I thought that was a good thing."

"Almost every cop in existence has had a complaint filed against him," Horowitz answered.

"It's a perk of the job," McNally added.

"At least half the time, it's a complaint that the punks got arrested in the first place," Horowitz added. "But you don't seem to even get those jokers. I'd almost suggest you don't do your job if it weren't for your arrest record."

I leaned back and shrugged. "I just talk to them."

"Talk to them?"

I nodded. "I make conversation. No reason not to. A lot of the guys we arrest aren't bad guys, just guys who do bad things. No reason not to talk to the parts that are still okay inside."

Horowitz arched a brow and looked at me like I was an alien. "People who talk like that generally don't like cops."

That got me to snicker. "Defense attorneys and Innocence Project idiots talk about the fundamental goodness of mass murderers, and they'll cry police brutality if the cuffs leave chafe marks. But if someone steals their TV, they'll demand the death penalty. It's guys on my end that understand criminals better." I gestured to my file, at one specific case. "Right there, for example, that Humphreys guy. Found him over his wife's dead body with the shotgun, crying over her, even though he killed her. Prosecution gave him less time than that Invernizzi guy, since guys who kill their spouse are less likely to do it ever again, even if they get married again. In Humphreys' case, he was sorry a few seconds after he did it. He was a good guy who did a bad thing but that doesn't mean we don't punish him."

"You deal with a lot of those 'good people'?" McNally asked.

"Everybody on the job does. It's just hard to see under the bullshit, when they're angry or jacked up. Get them calm enough, you can usually talk to them. The wannabe gangbangers south of Jamaica Avenue are harder to deal with, but I've come to an understanding with most of them."

I could see McNally's eyes light up with the prospect of getting me to confess to taking bribes. "Really?"

"Yeah. We're basically the old cartoon, with the sheepdog and the coyote? We come to work, we punch in, and we're antagonists. We punch out, we're just two guys coming from work. No reason not to treat them like people when they're not screwing around. We talk from time to time. Usually about the kids, girl troubles." I gave a sly smile. "Also, I've arrested one or two who talk to me like they forget I'm a cop."

McNally grinned. It was like it was the first thing I said that made me sound like a real cop. "They don't shut down after that?"

I smiled. How did one explain getting to a point where Mike Taylor could talk to me about his kids, and how he had to sell five pounds of marijuana to cover the latest iPhone for his daughter, then stopped, and we exchange a look akin to "I can't believe you said that."

"They know I catch them fair and square. Sometimes, they'll suddenly decide to become informants to buy a pass. Then we come by, fill out some CI paperwork, jump through some hoops, and we get a bigger fish. Sometimes, I arrest them, and they come along quietly, because they know I have them fair and square."

Sometimes, that would come with a good-natured smack upside the head, but I didn't want these two to decide that was police brutality.

"Interesting approach."

I shrugged. "I thought it was called community policing," I added. "They know me. I know them, and we all understand each other."

"And you get nothing from this relationship?"

I shrugged. "Sometimes, I do."

I admit, I was baiting them this time. Horowitz now looked like the hungry wolf who had a sniff of dinner. "Oh? How so?"

My PBA rep leaned over and reached a hand out to try to stop me from saying anything, but I answered, "They're always happy to give me a new criminal in the neighborhood. Crimes, dates, times, et cetera."

McNally: "You're arresting their competition?"

"Only for crimes they've done."

Horowitz: "Aren't you fostering the local criminal element instead?"

"I don't see it that way. I'd rather deal with the devil I know than waste time identifying newcomers. I know my crooks, and they know me."

McNally's eyes narrowed. "And what about Hayes, was he one of yours? Or did one of yours know him?"

"I wouldn't know," I answered honestly. "I haven't been out of the station house today. Even if I thought it was a good idea to talk to the guys on the street, I wouldn't want to text a photograph of Hayes all over the place. Before or after he died."

Horowitz nodded, either accepting my explanation, or confirming checkmate on the conversation. "Before the incident this morning, you claim that there was a smell in the station? And that the smell led you to Hayes?"

I nodded. "Yes," I added for the recorder. "Either it came from Hayes or something around him. Something may have died in the desk he was next to, or behind him. Hayes was covered in blood when he was arrested. We have our options."

"And you haven't smelled it afterwards? Even when Hayes was rolled out in a bag?"

I shook my head. "If it didn't come from Hayes himself, I presume that something had been thrown out in the general cleanup. That's what we've been doing all day."

McNally and Horowitz looked at each other, nodded, and rose. "Thank you, Detective Nolan, that will be all, I think," McNally said.

"You're probably clear. I don't think we'll have any more questions for you."

I cocked my head. That was sudden. "Why all the goodwill?"

Horowitz smiled as he flipped folders closed. "As you said, we punched in, we're antagonists. We're punching out on this one. Your collar from this morning, Mister Young, talked to us before we talked to you. He vouched for you."

I blinked, confused. *Anthony? Vouched for me?* "How so?"

McNally answered this time, as he packed his case. "He told us that Hayes attacked him during the fracas, and you saved him. The way he talked you up, you were Captain America and Superman rolled into one."

My eyebrows arched. I hadn't even considered that. "I'll stay with Clark Kent, thanks."

Horowitz looked to his partner. "Modest, too."

I shrugged. "Humility means being honest about yourself. I did no more than what anyone else in the room would have. And did. I didn't even stop him."

"I know," McNally replied. "But we're not all that concerned over it. We'll find out what drugs he was on after the toxicology comes back from the autopsy. We saw the body. He was anemic, malnourished, and scrawny—no way on God's Earth he was able to take on half the police station without a lot of help. We'll find out what chemicals, and we'll have a nice day. He has no family, and no one in the entire world to care whether he lives or dies."

I nodded. "Was that your analysis of the video?"

The two men from IA exchanged a look, and the bottom dropped out from my stomach. "What's the matter?"

Horowitz shrugged. "It's not important, but the cameras were on the fritz during the fight. Sometimes, it blinked out entirely; sometimes, it stayed on, but Hayes almost looked like he was flickering in and out of existence. It was strange."

"No, you think?" I snarked. "What about today wasn't strange?"

Chapter 4

HOME

I walked up to my brick-faced home and concentrated just enough to get the key in the lock. It was one of those days where I wish I took a car to and from work but that was usually when I was in a hurry to come home and collapse. The house was in the Glen Oaks community just north of Queens Village, about four blocks from the Easternmost border of New York City. If you missed the wrong turn, you'd accidentally end up in Nassau, in the *political* entity known as Long Island, as opposed to the physical, geographic location of Long Island, which included Queens and Brooklyn. You'd be surprised how many strange looks I get from fellow New Yorkers when I explained that four out of five boroughs were Islands, while the only part of New York City on the mainland was, of all things, the Bronx.

But Glen Oaks was a nice little neighborhood. It was an *ungated* community, isolated by design, with long blocks along main roads, but sprawling and twisting roads within. It came with its own underpaid security force (the job of which was to call the cops when the crap hit the fan), its own maintenance crews, and its own rabbit warren of streets, where, if you didn't know where you were going, you would disappear and never return ... at least, that's what I told my children, though adults believed it much more than the kids did.

My home was directly across the street from the security office, which was indistinguishable from the rest of the community, with the exception of the green awning over the doors.

At my dining room table—a round pedestal table that could have hosted a role-playing game or a board meeting—was my favorite person in the world, my wife Mariel. She had long, wavy chestnut brown hair, round, deep-brown eyes, a pleasant heart-shaped face, and a healthy olive complexion. As Ben Franklin would say, we fit well together.But the first person to tackle me with a hug was a woman I loved (no, not that way), but whose religious views I tolerated. Erin Quintanilla was a tall girl at 5'10", before the insanely high boots. Despite her last name, she had a complexion like Wednesday Adams, making her black hair pop. She was only mildly goth, with only a tiny diamond chip in her nose stud and only one or two visible tattoos. She also wore a big perky smile to go with her bubbly personality and a hug like an NFL player.

"Tommy! Tommy! Tommy!" she cried as she hugged-assaulted me. I didn't return the hug so much as I caught her on impact.

"Hey, Erin."

She landed on the ground with a *clomp*. "What's with the glitter?"

I looked over my body. There wasn't anything noticeable until I looked around on the floor. Glass had flown off of me on impact; I must have looked like a spectacularly gaudy Rockette outfit. "Nuts. Thought I got it all. Apologies. Guess I should shake out in the bathtub or something."

Mariel slipped in, hugging me. Her head just came up to my chest. I held her carefully against me (lest there was even more glass) and combed my fingers through her long wavy hair. "Hey."

"Hey, you. Heard there was some excitement at the station today."

"Guy went nuts. Guy went through a lot of windows. I'm now on first-name basis with the glazier *and* the vending machine guy."

Erin gaped. "Really? What are their names?"

"Eric and Jasyn—with a Y."

"What did the nut do that he was arrested for?" Mariel asked, still holding onto me. I wasn't in any rush to have her let go.

"Vagrancy, and being covered in blood. We think it wasn't human, but he went nuts before we could type every speck of blood on him."

Erin gave me a look that spoke volumes about her incredulity. "Where did they think the blood came from, then?"

"The animals around the park bench."

Erin slapped her hands over her mouth, eyes wide. "Oh no. Those poor little critters!"

Mariel took a step back to meet my eye. "Was anybody at the station hurt?"

Therein lies the difference between the two ladies—one focused on the squirrels, the other focused on my coworkers. Erin was "spiritual," a vague, uncertain term that always put teeth on edge.

"Mostly just roughed up. We got lucky. It could have been a lot worse. But it was a long tag-team match with a dozen men on one side and the nut on the other."

"Good. I don't look good in black," Mariel said, adding nothing more. She wore bright summer colors, yellow top and light blue jeans, while Erin was the one in solid black. Mariel and I had come to a decision long ago that Erin had wanted to be that goth character on *NCIS* when she grew up but missed a few details.

But Mariel's point was well taken. Since I'd been on the job, I'd been to one police funeral every few years but now to three and four a year. Our mayor wasn't helping the situation, deciding that he'd rather join Communist protesters at a G8 summit than go to a police funeral and throwing any and all support behind the cop killers—who were little better than common assassins. I could at least understand those criminals who fired off shots in the commission of a crime—that was usually a combination of fear and desperation. But two of the police killed had been deliberately assassinated, with the declaration that "Blue lives don't matter" by one of the killers. The last thing either one of us wanted was to attend another funeral.

I bent down and gave Mariel just a quick kiss on the lips—any more and we'd have to send our son Jeremy to go play down the block at his friend's house. "Aww," Erin drawled. "You two are just so *cuuuuttteee.*"

I arched a brow and just gave Erin *A Look*. "Puppies are cute. She is amazing. I'm...here."

Erin punched me in the arm. "Oh, you. You're just so cute together."

"Dad!"

Jeremy charged down the dining room to meet me, and even Erin had to get out of the way when he was running. He was only ten, but gaining height on his mother. He attacked my left side, hugging me around the waist. With Mariel on my right, and Erin hovering close by, I was very loved. Also, very crowded.

"Can I at least get my coat off, folks?"

"Oh! Right!" Jeremy exclaimed. He sped away, as though he needed to give me room on a landing strip.

I looked to Mariel. "And his teachers say he needs to be *more* sociable?"

"He doesn't interact with a lot of the other kids. Maybe one or two."

I shrugged out of my jacket and checked around the floor for more glass. None. "That may just be good taste on his part. It's easy to love humanity. Loving people is a little more difficult. This is said as someone who spends 90% of his day with the bottom 10% of the gene pool."

"Isn't that cynical?" Erin accused. "You still socialize with criminals."

"Yes. And a lot of them are good people with bad jobs." I pulled off my clip-on tie and popped the top button open. "But notice that I don't bring them home."

Mariel opened her mouth to disagree with me but closed it quickly. I knew she was going to crack my cynical facade by high-lighting some of the people I *had* brought home—mostly because they didn't have anywhere else to go. I don't like to advertise, mainly because people tend to blow it up bigger than it is—we have the room to put someone up for the night, so why not? It would be like giving me credit for feeding one of the neighborhood dogs with scraps; we won't use it, so why not hand it out? The only other option would be to get more stuff to use up the space.

Jeremy's problem, on the other hand, was more complicated. How? Because he had several enthusiastic pursuits that were unpopular at school. He couldn't talk about his range time because guns "upset some of the students" (IE: Upset one of the parents). Legos weren't "in" at the moment (who knew?). Trying to explain "Krav Maga" to *adults* could be problematic, to heck with children. I wasn't worried about him. The few friends Jeremy has are as close to true friends as one can get at his age.

After a few more minutes of small talk, Erin left. I was allowed to settle in at the table and lean back.

"Anything else happen today?" Mariel asked, handing me an iced tea.

"I ran in Young Anthony."

Mariel smiled. "I heard." I arched my brows, questioning, and she added, "Malinda called me during my time at the women's shelter, thanking *me* for *your* vigilance. Does the boy not do anything other than get caught? Does he enjoy getting caught?"

I shrugged. "Usually not. But as I implied to Erin, crooks are not necessarily the brightest bulbs. He snatched Malinda's purse *right* in front of me. He literally passed me to get to her." I shrugged. "People. What can you do?"

"Did you talk to him at all?"

"After a fashion. After the fight at the station today, Anthony seems to think I walk on water. Talked to me about doing right by everybody and doubling down on his studying. It was quite impressive."

"Not bad, Mister Policeman," she teased.

"I'll be happy if he does half of it." I frowned, confused. "Why is it that people are impressed by things like...that? Anthony acted like saving him was something extraordinary. It's like he doesn't understand that it's my job. Like I'm going to just let some psycho bite anyone's face off."

Mariel smiled at me. "And that you think it's something ordinary is one of the reasons why I love you."

I gave her a small smile. We'd had the conversation. She'd explained it to me before. One day, I hoped to understand her explanation.

I sagged into the chair. "Anything interesting happen while I dug through eight hours of bureaucracy?"

"Jeremy got into a fight at school," she said casually.

I started, sitting up straight. "He what? He started a fight?"

"He got into one. He didn't start it. Jeremy interceded."

I frowned. "What happened?"

"New kid named Ali decided to make his mark as lead bully. Jeremy objected."

I thought over my son's appearance. "Jerry didn't have any broken bones or bruises that I saw. What about the other guy?"

Mariel shrugged. "One hip throw was sufficient, apparently."

I took a drink. "I should probably ask, we sent Jerry to a Catholic school, right? When did Ali become a saint name?"

Mariel laughed. "We're literally in the most diverse corner of the planet Earth. We have a Buddhist temple a mile away, five Chinese restaurants within blocks of the school, and five store-front churches within six blocks. Good luck having a Catholic school that's even half Catholic."

I nodded slowly. "Remind me to look at the curriculum sometime soon. I'm sure that Jerry will be happy to tell me all about the fight over dinner."

And he was. I was almost certain that Jeremy had embellished a few details along the way. But he was cute about it. It basically boiled down to a hip throw to the floor, followed by a figure-four joint lock, seguing into a hammer lock. This is what happens when a cop's son gets Krav Maga lessons from an early age.

The final verdict from the school? Apparently, when a dozen children testify to a violent bully, even stupid school officials can come to the proper conclusion. I suspected that the bully would either be in jail within the next decade, or scared straight by the experience.

Dinner was just over when I got the call to report to a murder. This time, I could walk to the crime scene.

Chapter 5

WORKING THE CRIME SCENE

E ven though dispatch had given me the address, I didn't need it —I literally followed the lights and sirens, all the way to the block party of NYPD patrol cars parked all the way up and down the street. As I walked, I made note of what homes had cameras. While the little village we lived in had it's own security, it wasn't a gated community. And half a dozen Wi-Fi security cameras could be bought from CostCo for the price of a dinner out at Arby's for a family of five.

Before even seeing the slightest evidence of the crime, I knew it was going to be one of the least pleasant scenes I've been to. And yes, there is such a thing as a pleasant crime scene—a neat little twenty-two in the head, a touch of poison in the tea, or even a garrote around the neck.

The first rule of the crime scene is simple: When the Medical Examiner people are staying *outside*, away from the body, it's a bad one. In this case, they parked the ME van directly in front of the house, yet they were across the street, trying to get as far away from the scene of the crime without abandoning their van.

It got worse when I saw my partner, Alexander Packard, also standing outside. He was a tall, skinny fellow, bald with a graying handlebar mustache. His gray tweed was, as always, a size too large for him—it was as small as he could get before going to specialty stores for a size zero.

Packard had been in the navy, and had seen two crew mates eaten —one by a shark, one by a propeller—and had fifteen years on the job more than I did.

Packard gave me a wave, and I returned it "How did you get here so fast?"

He shrugged. "I was going to say hello. Congratulate you on meeting IA for the first time. Got the call on the way by."

I nodded and looked around at the usually orderly chaos of the neighborhood. "I'd ask how bad can it be, but..." I gestured to the ME van. "Is it that messy?"

"A real horror show. *And* the vic is thirteen."

I cringed. "Name?"

"Carol Whelan. Thirteen. She never made it to school. The parents work in the city, so they had to be up and out before she was even awake. She generally made it to the bus on her own."

I nodded. "The bus stop is only a block away. Where's school for her?"

"Grammar school down near the Cross Island. Saint Gregory the Great."

I sighed and shook my head. "God. My son goes to Greg's. She must have only been a year or two ahead of him. What happened to her?"

Packard frowned, stuck his hands in his pockets, and looked away. He stared off for a moment, and I was actually worried about him for a moment. My partner was perhaps the most sarcastic and cynical cop I knew in a profession that bred sarcastic and cynical.

Packard looked back at me with his deep blue eyes. "The question is more like what *didn't* happen to her.

"Obvious signs of cause of death include dismemberment and disarticulation."

I raised a brow. "Both? That seems like ... I can't tell if that's overkill or the most disorganized psycho ever."

"Embrace the power of 'and,' Tommy. From what the Medical Examiner guys could tell before they ran out of the room, most of the bones are broken, and the body cut to pieces at most of the major joints. It means ankles, knees, hips, wrists, elbows, shoulders, though he was at least nice enough to leave her head attached to her upper trunk."

I held out a hand. I didn't want to hear any more, and that was more than enough between now and the autopsy. "We can assume that he knows how to carve a turkey and wield a hammer. Got it. Time of death? Or did the ME not bother with a liver temperature before they ran out?"

"That would be difficult," Packard told me. "The liver isn't there."

I rolled my eyes. "Of course not. It wouldn't be a complete slasher film if the perp had left it behind. At this point, I'm just going to assume that there was a sexual component to this."

Packard shrugged. "That's the good news. For the moment, we can't tell. Our brave boys from the coroner couldn't hold onto their dinners that long. They say they're going to go in again in a few minutes. And that was a half-hour ago."

I sighed and shook my head. At the very least, I wasn't there for when they had discovered any of this nightmare. It was bad enough to hear about this without having to perform an in-depth examination to discover these horrors myself. "Now here's a real question: How did everyone beat me here? I literally walked to the crime scene, Alex."

He shrugged, and finally gave me a small, cynical smile that I knew him best for. "There was a debate about whether or not we should invite you in. We had to get hold of Statler and Waldorf to make certain that you were clear to work a crime scene already. Wouldn't want this guy to get off on a stupid technicality—though they're all stupid, really. This assumes he makes it to trial. Circulate the crime-scene photos around Rikers Island, I wouldn't lay money on him lasting long, unless he's in solitary the entire time." Packard's smile became evil. "But I'm told that's cruel and unusual punishment."

I gave him a flicker of a smile to show that I saw what he did there, but I wasn't in a mood to be amused. While I fully believed what I had told Internal Affairs that afternoon, and I knew that most of our perps were good people who did bad things, there were two exceptions that I had experienced: rapists, and people who committed crimes against children. It wasn't a coincidence that those two had the highest recidivism rate, and they seemed to be completely unrepentant. Funny enough, other criminals tend to enforce their own death penalty on them when they could.

"Anything else?"

Packard nodded. He pulled out his phone and flipped through a series of photographs. He picked one, played with the magnification, then showed it to me. "Then there was this."

I leaned forward. It was a photograph of the crown of Carol Whelan's head. She was apparently a brunette, but that was the only detail I could make out about her. The picture was focused on what looked like a large-bore needle mark in the girl's head, and possibly her skull. "What the hell?"

"Your guess is as good as mine, Tommy."

I frowned. This was the "cleanest" part of the murder, from what was described, and the most puzzling. Then again, it was like there were two killers: one was precise and methodical, who made incisions to disarticulate joints and used a needle; and a second killer who was violent, deranged, and broke bones apart.

"It's too much to hope for fingerprints left in a pool of blood?" I asked.

Packard pulled back the phone. "Yup. Even though he did enough finger painting."

I blinked. *Did I miss a memo?* "Explain, please?"

"Oh, right, the Jackson Pollock in her blood. One second." He flipped through the photographs on the phone again, then handed it back to me. "Make like it's Tinder and swipe right."

I did. It was like Packard had made it just for me. There were no images of Carol Whelan, but there were plenty of the walls. I presumed that the red and black "paint" was her blood.

There was a circle with some spikes coming out of it, and what looked like a hand with an apple being thrust at the circle. There was no reason I could think of, but the image left me cold. The next one looked like squiggles, though it could have been a language that didn't use the Latin script. The third image was a triangle with lines coming out of it, and an oval in the middle. It looked like a bizarre child's drawing, with art materials prepared by Stephen King. The last and final one looked like nothing so much as a demonic cow, complete with horns. If the circle and apple left me cold, this dropped the temperature to "sub-zero."

"He's not getting into art school, that's for certain," I drawled. I made certain to text the relevant photos over to my phone and then handed Packard his. "Has anyone checked the organs? Or is that also something the ME didn't get around to yet?"

"The latter. But I can't blame them. This is one meat puzzle I wouldn't want to assemble."

"Any sign of forced entry?"

"None. Windows are shut tight. Doors were locked. The parents had to unlock the front door with a key."

I winced. "Which one found her?"

"Both."

I nodded, and turned towards the house. It was time to head inside. "Shall we?"

Packard put away the phone, and we went inside.

I did my best and did not gag with the scent of blood the moment I opened the door. In fact, there was no decay in the air, which I would have expected, given everything that Packard had told me.

I will spare you the gorier details on the corpse of young Carol Whelan. It was indeed a mess. The only relevant detail is the layout of her remains. Each part that had been disarticulated was itself split in half. Each piece was carefully laid on the floor like she had been laid out on a bed, or a slab in the morgue. But there was nearly an inch of space between each part, just to show that they had been separated.

This was perhaps the neatest, most organized crazy person ever.

The second relevant detail ... the floor was wall-to-wall carpet, so we all needed to slip paper coverings over our shoes, just to make certain that we didn't tread blood all over the place. It was probably too late, but minimizing contamination was a real hazard. I was trying to reconcile how much blood had soaked the carpet with how much was on the wall. Who knew she had so much blood in her?

"So, no signs of forced entry," I said, examining the living room.

"No signs of sexual assault," Packard added, "for the moment— let's face it, a black light will make most of the floor light up with blood, if nothing else."

I stood at the edge of the living room and just felt the air for a moment. "Warm in here, isn't it?"

Packard nodded. "Good catch. The thermostat has been raised to over ninety. The mother says that it was at sixty-five when they left. And no, no prints on it."

I frowned. He had raised the temperature deliberately. Did he just like it warm? Did he use it as a forensic countermeasure, trying to screw up the temperature of the body? Was the lack of liver a similar countermeasure? After all, he had taken the trouble to cut up the body, why not take some liver home while he was at it?

"I smell blood, but shouldn't something like decomp have started already?"

Packard shrugged. "Could have. Hasn't. And if it's been this hot since before eight—the parents say she leaves at quarter to—then you'd figure it would have."

I looked to Packard with a sickening thought. "Think she could have been alive only a few hours ago?"

"That's what I'm thinking. Especially with the blood. Some of it isn't dry on the walls yet. That won't be confirmed until later."

I tightened my lips together to keep from throwing up. "I know one way to test."

I took out my tactical baton, and carefully flicked it open to make certain that I didn't hit anything or anyone. I approached the edge of the visible pool of blood. I reached over and slid the tip of the baton under one of her delicate little fingers, and lifted. Her finger moved easily. I stepped back, wiped at my baton with a Wet Nap (you'd carry them, too, in my line of work), and held it against my arm. These things were a pain to close unless you were smacking them against concrete.

"Not stiff yet," Packard observed, which was the point. "Not even four hours."

Which meant that I was having dinner with my family while little Carol was still being murdered. Also, that the killer had prevented her from leaving for school twelve hours ago, yet she was still alive less than four hours ago. I didn't need a medical examiner or forensics to make a guess about how this bastard spent his time.

No, I wasn't feeling particularly generous.

I closed my eyes, ran through a quick prayer, and took a slow breath...

And then I caught the whiff of something foul and vile. It was worse than the smell of blood, and cut through everything else that had assaulted my nose since I came in. Yes, it is common to use a sort of menthol gel, or even vapor rub under the nose to block out the smell at crime scenes, but I dislike the practice, lest I miss something.

In this case, I'm surprised I even caught this. It was faint, and barely there, almost like I was undergoing an odorous hallucination, which would be a first for me, and possibly most other people.

The strange thing was that it smelled familiar.

"Hold on a sec, Alex," I said to Packard. "Give me a moment."

I followed my nose, and moved slowly and carefully through the crime scene. I worked my way around the body, and made certain that when I arrived at the other side, I hadn't tread any blood with me. I hunted the scent, and kept my hands in my pockets the whole time. I was deathly afraid of messing up the evidence trail; I wanted to make certain that when we got this bastard, we threw him into the deepest hole we could find. Yes, repentance and forgiveness are part of the faith, but step one is that he must repent.

I traced it upstairs, into Carol's room. It was very pink, from the walls and ceiling to the carpet. There didn't seem to be any drag marks or heavy impressions left in the carpet, but I still kept one eye on the carpet, while following the stench to the its source.

The closet door was partially open, and the smell seemed to emanate from inside.

I took my hands out of my pocket, and unsnapped my holster, keeping one hand on my gun. I reached forward, hooked the open door with my elbow, and pulled back on it.

The murder weapon was stabbed into the middle of the closet's back wall. And into the wall was carved: "Come and get me, Patron Saint of Detectives."

I don't know why, but at that moment, I realized that I knew where the smell had come from: that morning, at the station, right before the altercation with Hayes. It was the same smell ... even though Hayes was dead at the same time that Carol Whelan was being murdered.

Chapter 6

BEATING THE BUSHES

Everyone knows Sherlock Holmes' famous saying that once you exclude the impossible, whatever remains, no matter how improbable, must be the truth. I am, however, unaware of Sherlock needing to deal with a scent distinctive to a dead man. But I was still left with the distinctive rotting scent that is distinctive to a dead man. So unless he had a family that had decidedly horrific body odor (that only I could smell) as a genetic defect, it was probably just a coincidence. Hayes had no family—IA had told me that during the interview.

I took a few photographs of the closet and the message carved into the wall. I called CSU to come upstairs and be careful along the way. No one was going to disturb the crime scene if possible, even though we'd all disturbed it the moment the door was opened.

Packard was waiting for me at the bottom of the stairs. I pointed outside, and we didn't say a word as we made it through the door. I handed him my phone with the photo of the closet on the screen and told him where I found it.

"Patron Saint of what?" Packard handed returned the phone. "Any idea what it means?"

I shrugged. "No idea. We Papists have a patron saint of cops: as the prayer goes, St. Michael the Archangel, defend us in battle. But no detectives that I'm aware of."

"I'd say Daniel," Packard said. "He had a nice trick with flour and three old guys. But I don't recall him being a Saint."

"Ditto."

Packard sighed. "Great. Aren't you glad they don't let just anyone into your neighborhood? Only the Grade AAA plus psychos are allowed to kill here." He jerked his head off to one side. "Want to talk to the parents? They're over at the security office. They didn't want to stay in the house."

Across the street from my house. "Can't blame them."

"Not sure about that," Packard snarked. "If they took their daughter to school, she'd still be alive."

I would excuse his behavior as a result of working the murder of a child, but that would be a lie. After decades of man's inhumanity towards man, Packard was always this grouchy. He once told me that his parents had declined to call him Richard because "We were never rich before, why should the family start with me being Rich?" He went on for a few paragraphs in a comedy routine that would make Jackie Mason go "Oy."

The security office wasn't very big, just enough for a front desk, and some locker rooms on a lower floor. One section in the back was a retrofitted living room that looked like a break room for five, but only if one person stood at a time.

In a back corner sat Briana and Keiran Whelan. Keiran was tall and tan, with a little gray in his five o'clock shadow. Briana was a big busty blonde with wide, high cheekbones and wide blue eyes. They were both beautiful people who looked like a train had crashed through their lives. On the way over, Packard had given me some background. They were a nice power couple who ran their own ad agency and hurt no one. They weren't millionaires, but they were comfortable.

During the interview, it was exactly what you'd expect. It was as tough as an interrogation of the average street thug but worse, because even the gentlest question was apt to set off another round of crying from one parent or the other. I didn't mention the joys of Heaven, or the glory of God's embrace, because nothing would have been a comfort. Keiran acquitted himself well, but even he had to stop every now and again to pull himself together. Briana held up for an average of three questions before she had to cry. It was even difficult for Packard, who was as empathetic as a tree trunk.

Carol had been the youngest child of three. The first was away at college, being trained to become a Master of the Universe, the second was working his butt off at the CIA—the Culinary Institute of America up in Dutchess County—and Carol was the baby. She had been named Carol because she had been born in December, and Dickens was on in the background (the Muppet version, with Michael Caine, if that matters). With the innocent solipsism of the average child, growing up, she thought that *A Christmas Carol* was all about her.

No, there were no personal enemies. There were no spiteful, angry and jealous relatives seething with resentment, as both parents were only children, with no close living relatives. If a family member was involved, it would require distant relatives from California creaking out of their retirement homes to enact vengeance out of a Gothic novel. We would beat the bushes in that direction, but unless there was a scorpion lurking in the bush that used to be the family tree, it was unlikely. It was also a pain in the ass, since that sort of thing was the most likely source of killers—statistically, most human beings who are murdered are going to be murdered between two and four in the morning by their nearest and dearest. With the parents excluded (Packard had done so with a phone call) and no relatives, a great big chunk of the usual suspects were right out the window.

What friends were in the neighborhood? Who cleaned the house? Any creepy friends who they wouldn't let their kids around? No, all of their nearby friends (who actually lived within driving or train-trip distance) were at a bash out in the Hamptons for the week while it was still warm—if Carol hadn't had school, or if she had been older, the Whelans would have gone to the party. Keiran, especially, had considered taking Carol along so they could get in tennis before it became too cold ... but Carol had been the one to insist that she had to go to school to see all of her friends.

At that comment, all four of us had to take a ten-minute timeout.

When we came back from our brief adjournment, it was time for another tack. How about professional enemies? Professional enemies were always a good thought.

Strangers? Sex fiends in the neighborhood? I didn't even ask, since I knew the answer—I lived a few blocks away, with a child, and me being a cop, trust me, I kept tabs on that sort of thing. There was no one who lived or worked in the area. Of course, that meant nothing if a predator came out of his comfort zone so he could stalk fresh prey.

But you could start to see our problem. They had relatives, and we had to make sure that all of the relatives that they knew about had stayed in their corner of the country, *and* make sure that some random apple that nobody noticed hadn't dropped out of the tree and rolled off into a corner. They say they don't know about any business rival or colleague who could or would have done this, but who knows what evil lurks in the hearts of men? And who knows if any random nut on the street had spotted Carol one day and took a depraved fancy to her?

And we had to work *all* of those angles.

If you've ever done research into how real-life murder investigations work, they range from easy to impossible. Easy was, as I said, being murdered by the nearest and dearest in the bedroom. More difficult was the one where the killer was an acquaintance or a friend, or even a slightly distant relative—this is what most murder mysteries boil down to, be it at a dinner party out in the country, or trapped in a locked train car filled with suspects. Solving those crimes boils down to the ancient question of *Cui Bono*? Who benefits? After that, it starts to get more difficult. The reason so many murders go unsolved is because there are so many strangers killing strangers —be they serial killers, a street mugging, or a hired gun from out of town. The impossible is the hired gun from out of town, since they're flown in just for the killing and fly out after the job is done.

As you've read, we had excluded *a lot* of possibilities. Some were still possible—sure, a friend could have slipped the leash of the week-long Hampton party and come out to cosplay as Jeffrey Dahmer. There was a Long Island Rail Road station within an hour's walking distance, so it was possible. But was it *likely*? Not really. There was no hangover that could last long enough for someone to go missing from the Hamptons for over twelve hours (a four-hour round trip, and eight hours of violence). Second possibility: a business rival or colleague who harbored a secret resentment of both Keiran and Briana that they were totally unaware of. Was it truly likely? Not really, unless it was someone really unstable who decided that his true ambition in life was to play Iago. The out-of-town assassin was also thrown right out the window—no one who could be considered professional would be this much of a butcher.

The nightmare scenario was "the total and complete stranger." Unfortunately, in this day and age, it no longer had to be someone local. If Carol had been in a photograph or a video put on social media, anyone within flying distance could be a suspect—again, highly improbable, but not impossible. If the killer were a total stranger, we would need to be lucky, with the parking ticket or the fake nickel, or any other famous clue that led to the apprehension of a spy or a killer. The worst part here is the other cliché mystery authors made use of: we would have to hope that *this* killer screwed up. Massively. We would have to hope for DNA, and that he was in the system. Or that he removed his gloves, or there was a surface he failed to wipe down. Worst case scenario, we would have to hope that he screwed up at the *next* crime scene.

You can see why we *hope* that this was done by someone they knew: a narrow pool of suspects was comparatively easy.

Before you ask yourself, "Tommy mentioned security cameras earlier. What happened to that angle?" That angle died during the interview, when I got a text message that reported no security cameras within two blocks of the crime. That may seem like only a start, but there were more small winding paths through the neighborhood than even I could count. If there wasn't a camera close by, the killer could have come from almost any direction.

Three hours of questions, prodding, and poking at the relationships of all the Whelans—Keiran, Briana, Carol, and both of their sons—and we were finished. I will give them this, they held up. They broke down a few times – I nearly broke down a few times, and so did Packard – but they endured every question we had, and I offered a continuation at a later date once every thirty minutes. They took the opportunity for a brief break, but they both insisted that they answer every question we had.

By the time we left, it was after midnight, and the Whelans were going to check into a hotel. I offered to contact their son at the CIA to make certain that he didn't come home into this mess. When I tried calling him, the interference was so heavy, I couldn't call out. Packard called out on his phone, and handed it to me...and it stopped working for me as well. Packard took over the notifications, and said, "Maybe your hot-line to Heaven is causing interference."

"Funny."

"Yes, I am."

It was time to really get to work. As most TV shows will inform you, the first 48 hours of the investigation is the most important. After that, evidence gets wiped away by the weather, time, and just people who could carry physical evidence on their shoes. Witnesses forget things, and we had to find these witnesses before they forgot anything.

But in this case, we had the canvass started. Every house in the neighborhood was being canvassed by uniforms (except for mine; I could ask Mariel myself).

One of the first things I did, once we were settled in the car, was to call Erin Quintanilla. Packard had to call and put it on speaker, since my phone still didn't want to work for me.

As the phone rang, Packard asked, "You sure she's going to be up at this hour?"

"She's so Goth I'm surprised she goes out in daylight," I answered.

There was a click, though there was a lot of static. She still sounded so damn perky. "Tommy? What are you doing up at this hour? You're not working, are you?"

"Kinda. Listen, Erin, how did you get to my house today?"

"I went up Little Neck Boulevard, hung a left at the first stop sign, and went straight to your place. Why?"

I frowned. That was the wrong path for her to have seen anything. "How about the way out?"

"Same path, just the other way...why do you ask? Did something happen?"

"There was a crime in the neighborhood."

Erin gave a humorless laugh. "Crime. Tommy, you're homicide. Who died?"

"A kid. Carol Whelan. Do you know the name? The family?"

"Nope. Sorry. Did you ask Mariel? Even Jerry?"

I winced at the thought of my son knowing this girl. "Not yet. They're on the list."

"Okay. But if it helps, I didn't see anyone aside from the little old people who really want me to run them over."

I smiled a little. One of the problems with Glen Oaks was that there were a surplus of little old folks who took their sweet time going from point A to point B. They do it so often, I half-suspected that they deliberately crossed in the middle of the street and wore black as soon as the sun went down. They either wanted people to hit them or wanted to be traffic hazards. Either way, I understood what Erin meant.

"Anything else?" Erin asked.

"No. If I have anything else, I'll call you."

"That's one mark checked off of the list," Packard muttered. "Any other blind alleys you can think of?"

"Sure. Want to type this into VICAP?"

For those who don't know, the Violent Criminal Apprehension Program (or ViCAP) is part of the FBI out of Quantico that analyses things like Carol's murder—serial violent and sexual crimes. It was originally started to track serial killings via their signatures; things left behind that are distinctive and unique to the killer himself. The

FBI gave the VICAP database, used by cops across the country to compile data on sex crimes, missing persons, and homicides. Local cops entered data from these cases into the system and the data is compared to other cases in an attempt to make connections.

There's a major drawback with the system, though: Cops have to enter their cases into the system. If they don't, VICAP has nothing to go on. If a killer kept themselves in the right precincts, ones that kept their records on paper and never digitized them, then he could avoid detection for years.

You may wonder why I refer to the killer as male. The likelihood of Carol's killer being a woman are so low, I'd have to be a mathematician to give you an accurate answer.

Since I drove, Packard had to access VICAP via his phone, because, of course, there was an app for that. It would take forever to search the whole system with a phone keyboard, but dismemberment AND disarticulation were distinct search terms. And we would have more terms to search by when we were at a real keyboard, checking off all the boxes and dotting all the i's.

VICAP came up with no results.

A geographic search for recently released degenerates came up empty, which surprised me. I would have figured there would have been one closer than five miles, but there were a lot of school zones in the area. The nearest cluster of them were south of Jamaica Avenue. That gave us something, but probably not in the way you're thinking.

I pulled up at a street corner at Hempstead Turnpike and 222nd street, a little over a mile from the station house. The corner had a "massage parlor" that gave out specific massages and also dealt other "medicinal herbs" that were technically legal. Yes, we knew about it, but as these things went, they were the least of a few dozen devils that we could name you.

The owners of the establishment were outside on the corner. My conversation with IA included the casual talks with crooks I knew. The owners were said people. They were crooks who saw crime as a business. It was how they made their money. They were borderline respectable. They dressed in black, with leather jackets, but their black shirts were professional, button down collars with the top button undone. Their pants were professional, with a few scattered black jeans, and most importantly, they wore belts and wore their pants up around their waists.

I parked the car at the corner and stepped out, leaving Packard in the car. I headed for the biggest, blackest guy on the corner.

"Hey, D."

"D" was Daniel David DiLeo. Someone tried calling him 3D once, and the ensuing brawl quickly put a stop to that nickname. He nodded at me, then continued surveying the street. " 'Sup, Detective?" he rumbled in a voice like a base drum.

To my recollection, he had never called me by name, only my rank. "Bad night. Have a second?"

"Probably."

I took out my phone, and called up a photograph of Carol Whelan back when she was a beautiful, happy, lively young girl. D spared me a glance and shrugged. "Am I supposed to know her?"

"She's my victim," I replied. I slid the phone away. "I'll spare you the 'after' photo."

"And this has what to do with me?"

"The area is littered with school zones," I told him. "Therefore all the people we might like for this have clustered into certain areas. One of the larger clusters is in your area of operations."

D's face become dark and menacing, with his brow furrowed so deeply, it looked like a dent in his skull. "Really?" he drawled. "Well, then, I'm going to have to look into that."

I held up a hand. "All I'm asking is that you keep an ear open for anything you or your men might hear."

"Can't promise my boys won't take matters into their own hands."

I sighed. I couldn't figure out the business model D wanted to take inspiration from—Hell's Angels, the Zetas, or Michael Corleone. The situation wasn't helped by D having a little girl with one of his girlfriends in the neighborhood. "Try to avoid a situation that would put me on your case, D, would you? You need to be out to tend to Julie. Let me handle it."

D grimaced. "You say so."

I tried to give him a reassuring smile. "Don't worry about it. Put him in general population at Rikers, you might get the end result you desire anyway."

D nodded. I didn't have to connect the dots for him. He knew Carol had to be dead because I was on the case. Pederasts and child killers were in season all year round in jail and in prison. They tended to herd together for protection, because being separated from the herd on the South African veldt was safer than being separated from the pack behind bars.

"How is Julie, anyway?"

D smiled slightly. "She's doing good. Spelling whole words. Going straight to cursive. Pity she can't be a doctor. Handwriting's too good."

I grinned. "That's wonderful. Tell her to keep it up. I—"

I was suddenly hit with a whiff of something familiar. It wasn't the scent of Hayes or from the crime scene, but similar enough that it caused me to turn around.

A car was pulling up to the curb, heading the wrong direction, so the driver opened his door and stepped onto the sidewalk. I took two steps towards the car, and the driver reached inside his jacket as he saw me. I lengthened my stride so that it was two long steps, and I kicked the door closed, slamming him between the door and his car. I threw my shoulder into the door, keeping him and his arm pinned. I met his face with the blade of my forearm, and reached down his open side to grab what he was looking for. Unsurprisingly, it was a gun, a nice little MP5K-PDW sub-machinegun.

"Lovely," I drawled. I leaned harder on the door and in the newcomer's face, and looked at D. "Friend of yours?"

D frowned, studying him. "Hard to see with your arm in his face."

The perp reached down with his free hand, and came out with a knife, point down, like an ice pick. He raised it over his head, and I hammer-fisted his elbow and held it there, driving the arm back. I was joined by Packard, who had leaped out of the car when the fight started, as well as D himself, holding the left arm. D yanked down at the sleeve, and revealed a mess of tattoos that even I recognized.

"MS-13," I griped. "Wonderful." I glanced to D. "There something I should know?"

He shrugged. "They asked to sell in our territory. We told them no. We want nothing to do with these people."

My partner glanced at D. "And you thought they'd take no for an answer?"

D shrugged. "That was a week ago. They're usually not that patient."

"But do they usually stink this much?" I asked.

Packard cuffed the gunman, then gave me a look like I was crazy, a look that D matched.

"What are you talking about?" Packard asked.

D nodded. "No idea what you mean."

Is my nose broken? I thought. *Can't be, I smelled this guy before I heard or saw him.*

I glared at this idiot. "This is going to cost me time I don't have to book your sorry behind, dumb ass. Hope you're happy."

By the time the MS-13 idiot had been processed, it was dawn. He was cuffed, Mirandized, printed, identified (he didn't want to talk to us, and didn't have any ID on him), booked, and sent into the system with our blessing. He was one Rene Ormeno, with a dozen warrants out on him for child prostitution, trafficking in children, murder, rape, racketeering, conspiracy, witness tampering, et al. Given how many different crimes he was wanted for, we decided it would be a good thing if he was lost in the system for a day or two before anyone else was alerted to his presence. All we needed was one idiotic judge who decided that Ormeno could be released on his own recognizance, and he would be in the wind ... if you think that's not possible, I will merely inform you that the history of the New York City judiciary includes a man nicknamed "Turn 'em loose Bruce."

But the momentum of the case was slowed shortly thereafter with phone calls. For some reason, every time I wanted to make a call to keep the case moving forward, I got static or poor reception. Every time some paper pusher wanted to talk about the arrest—be they lawyers, bureaucrats who wanted Ormeno in the system *right this minute*, and at least two calls from the US Marshal service who wanted Ormeno's head on a platter for crimes in another state—I had crystal clear reception. I couldn't even call home when I tried—four times over the course of the day. Anything I wanted to get done by phone had to be done by text—and that was 50-50—or my partner had to do it.

By 8:00 that evening, we had made no headway on the case. None. We had ruled out the friends at the Hamptons party by speaking to each one on the phone in turn, and there was enough overlap that they were all alibied for our window of opportunity, unless a minimum of three people were in on it. We had to drive 15 miles into Manhattan to talk to the Whelans' employees. Not one of them could consider the possibility that one of their coworkers, or one of their competitors, could have been involved—and every employee had been in yesterday for a staff meeting. With traffic, that was six hours of the day wasted.

The most productive use of our time that day was our trip to Hempstead Turnpike. There had been a sudden spike in arrests that day for possession of child porn or perverts found in school zones. The only thing they all had in common was that they were all in D's area of operation.

As I told IA, a lot of criminals are good people who do bad things.

I got home at 8:30 that evening. I had Packard drive me home, and he was happy to do it. This was one of the few times we had ever "given up" on an investigation this early. No, we weren't going to consider this case a lost cause until we worked it to death, or worked ourselves to death. But after a 24-hour day, where we didn't even have a viable suspect, we decided to turn in and try again tomorrow.

My front door opened as soon as I closed Packard's car door. Mariel was there and rushed out of the house to hug me. I caught her, and, unlike with Erin's tackle-hug the day before, I fell back against Packard's car and had to push myself straight.

"Tough day?" I asked.

"Jerry came home crying. They waited for the end of the day, right before the last period. Who does that? I mean, it was just dropped on them, and they had Father Ryan come in and talk to them, and I don't even think that they were going to tell anyone if they could have avoided it, like they could have hidden it away from the entire school, or maybe even the entire parish, and—"

I held up my hand in surrender, one arm still around her. "Avoided what? Waited to do what?"

Mariel closed her eyes, and tried not to cry. "One of Jeremy's friends was murdered, Tom. He's already cried himself to sleep over it. She was an older girl, named Carol Whelan. She was killed just down the street... what is it?"

Chapter 7

BUMP IN THE NIGHT

I awoke to the sound of my child screaming in terror. I was halfway out of my bedroom door before I knew I was awake. I flipped the lights on in his room. His back was flat up against the headboard, his feet up against his pillow, his hands gripping the top of the headboard, as though he were going to climb up the wall backwards. I glanced at the bed, the floor, the ceiling, in case it was a spider, or a rat. Those threats ruled out, I went straight for him and caught him as he flung himself at me. I wrapped my arms around him, and he held onto my neck tight enough that I was a little concerned about being strangled.

"It's okay, Jerry, I'm here, buddy. I'm here. What's the matter? Bad dream? Monster in the—"

And then I caught it. That odor again. The smell of Hayes, and the Whelan crime scene, and to a lesser extent, Rene Ormeno. Whatever it was that tied those three together had been *in my house*, in my son's bedroom.

"Was it the smell?" I asked, calmer, and probably less reassuring than I should have been.

"No. I-it was Ca-Carol!" he sobbed.

I almost sighed in relief. A nightmare about a murdered classmate wasn't unexpected. It was certainly more rational than half the nightmare scenarios running through my brain.

"Sh-she was all-all-all cut up," he continued. "She was in pieces, but still held together. There was this big hole in her head, and her skin was carved up. And she tried to touch me in a bad place."

That made my blood run cold.

I reached down to the bedsheet, and pulled it straight. And there, on the center of the sheet, was a perfectly-shaped, bloody little hand print.

"You're staying in bed with me and Mommy tonight, okay, champ?"

"Oh-oh-oh-kay."

I felt someone behind me, and I glanced. I made out Mariel's form at the edge of my vision. "What's wrong?"

"He saw Carol," I told her gently, almost as a whisper, so Jeremy couldn't hear me over his crying and screaming.

Mariel's bleary eyes widened, and then again. I think it took her a moment to parse my phrasing. Not that he thought he saw Carol but that he saw the dead girl I had seen the night before.

She mouthed, "What's going on?"

I shrugged and handed Jeremy over to her. I leaned in with him between us. I kissed her on the cheek, then whispered in her ear, "When I know, you will. Take him to bed? I'll be right there."

She nodded and went back to our bedroom without another word.

I turned back to the bedroom and stepped inside. The smell of death and decay was slowly fading, but it was still nauseating. But Mariel hadn't commented on it, and Jeremy hadn't said anything when I asked him about it.

At a glance, everything was still in place. The *Lord of the Rings* posters were still up on the wall—*Return of the King,* and one with Liv Tyler as Arwen, so he had taste—with a pile of books on his night table. Both were fine. His closet door was propped open by a half-finished Lego Death Star. Above his dresser was a light blue paper target with holes in it from the range.

It was perfect. Nothing was touched, except for the bed.

I flattened the bed sheet again. The hand print was still there. I leaned closer to examine it and was hit with a stronger stench. It seemed to be the only source left in the room. I picked Jeremy's flip phone off of his nightstand, took a photo of the hand, texted it to my phone, and Packard's phone, then wiped it from Jeremy's. I didn't expect the hand print to go anywhere, but I wanted evidence of it while I was awake.

I glanced over my shoulder and backed out of Jeremy's bedroom, closing the door as I went. I wasn't going to take any chances. I proceeded to check every door and window in the house. It took a while, but they were secured.

I got back to my bedroom. The overhead light was on. Jeremy was already in bed with Mariel. I caught her attention, my hand at the light switch. She nodded and reached over to the nightstand lamp. She turned the lamp on as I turned off the overhead light. I closed the door behind me and slid into bed. Jeremy turned and held me tightly.

"She was a friend of mine, Dad," he told me. "Someone killed her."

"I know. I'm going to find him, Jerry."

Jeremy brightened. "You're going to catch him, Dad? You going to shoot him?"

While Jeremy was one of the more enlightened children in New York on the subject of firearms, he still had the bloodthirsty nature of the average boy. "If I have to."

"Good."

We turned off the light, and settled into bed. I glanced at the clock on top of the bookcase—placed there so we would have to actually get out of bed to turn off the alarm—it was 11:30. It had been 10:59 when I had closed my eyes and finally wound down enough to sleep.

I closed my eyes and drifted to sleep...

Stomp. Stomp. Stomp.

I was awake and out of bed, opening the drawer of my nightstand before I realized it. I looked at the ceiling.

Stomp. Stomp. Stomp. Stomp. Stomp.

I drew my gun from the nightstand. Somebody was in my attic, running laps.

Stomp. Stomp. Stomp. Stomp. Stomp. Stomp.

Mariel turned the light on, and I held out my hand, signaling both her and Jeremy to stay where they were.

I cracked the door open, and spied outside, just to make certain that no one was in the hallway. I swung out, gun ready, and made my way to the attic stairs.

Stomp. Stomp. Stomp. Stomp. Stomp. STOMP. STOMP. STOMP. STOMP.

I quietly cracked the attic door open.

STOMP. STOMP. STOMP. STOMP. STOMP. STOMP. STOMP.

I could feel the vibrations in my chest. I had the sucker pinned.

I burst up the stairs, and swept over it with my weapon. "Freeze, sucker."

Dead silence.

I reached for the pull chain for the overhead light and yanked it. The lights went on, and the entire attic was empty. There was no one. Nothing. Even the dust was undisturbed—except for my footprints, the dust balls were pretty much the way they were last time I was there. I would have done an in-depth search, but there was nothing to search. There was an old cabinet and a closet, and I checked both.

And there was still that smell of dead filth.

"Seriously, what the Hell is going on?" I muttered. I frowned, turned the light out, and made my way back down stairs.

My heart was racing, breathing accelerated, and I felt like I was going to have a heart attack. I did a sweep of the house again, walking the entire building, every floor and every room, even the basement. My heart raced the entire time.

I frowned in thought, and I wore the expression all the way back to the bedroom. I found Mariel had her own gun from her nightstand in one hand, the other arm around our son.

"Well?" she asked.

"Did you arrest it, Daddy?" Jeremy insisted eagerly.

I closed the door behind me and flipped the latch on it. "There was nothing," I said, putting my gun back in the nightstand. "Nothing."

Both Mariel and Jeremy looked at me like they didn't quite believe me.

"You're kidding," she said, her voice like lead. "You can't be serious."

I slipped back into bed. Doors and windows locked. There was nothing else I could do, unless I was going to suggest that we pack up all three of us and move into a hotel for the night—and I couldn't imagine a hotel more secure than my house, with a security station literally across the street. Also, I don't think the local Howard Johnson's would have appreciated my bringing my shotgun, and Mariel's rifle, in addition to the sidearms.

Mariel turned off the light, and the three of us cuddled together. All was quiet, except for my beating heart. It hadn't slowed from the moment the footsteps stomped in the attic until I came back to the bed. I had no problem with being shot at in the middle of the street, or arresting a mid-level MS-13 psycho like Rene Ormeno, and even a random traffic stop scared me less than that, and it was the most dangerous police duty. But something in my home, threatening my family? Completely different

I glanced at the clock. It was 11:45, I had been up for 36 hours, and I still hadn't slept.

It took an hour for my system to stop buzzing with anxiety. It took more time for my body to just give in to the exhaustion.

Then the phone rang.

I started awake, surprised. My phone had been noncompliant all day, giving me nothing but static and garbled noise, and *now* it decided to get crystal clear reception? Argh. I reached over, grabbed it, and turned it on.

"Lleh fo serif eht ni nrub uoy hctaw dna luos rouy laets ot gniog ma I."

I frowned at it, put it on silent, and slapped it back down on the nightstand. Either it was gibberish, or I couldn't string together the meaning. Either way, it could wait until morning. My phone saved conversations, just in case we needed the record later. Maybe the tech guys at TARU could help on that one.

I curled up back to sleep. The phone had read that it was 1:05 AM. I was allowed to drift back to sleep faster this time, since I was no longer scared out of my mind by jump scares from a horror film.

I was startled back to full awareness with a sudden chill. Despite being under the blankets, it felt like I was naked and out in the cold during winter. It was only September, so even an open window wouldn't have explained it.

The chill didn't only hit me. Even Jeremy shivered and curled up against me. Mariel rolled over, and reached for the heavier blanket at the foot of the bed. Figuring out what she had in mind, I sat up to grab the blanket.

There was a giant shadow at the foot of the bed. Not a person, just a shadow as wide as the bed, with arms, legs, a head near the ceiling. It seemed to fill the room.

Mariel gasped, which woke up Jeremy, who screamed, and I grabbed my gun.

By the time I turned back with my pistol, the shadow was gone.

"Okay, Tommy, what the Hell was that?" Mariel gasped. "And don't tell me it was just a trick of the light."

I frowned, reached over, turned on the light. "I can't tell if we need an exorcist or Ghostbusters."

"I'm good with either."

I put my gun down, leaving it on the night stand and not in the drawer. I wasn't going to be messing around the next time something happened, and I was going to assume that it was.

It was now two in the morning.

Jeremy clung to my arm, and I tried to give him a reassuring smile. I grabbed a rosary from my nightstand drawer, rolled over under the blanket, and started going through the rosary with him. We started with the *Our Father*, and we only said the Hail Mary seven or eight times before the repetition sent us to sleep.

This time, we slept straight through the night.

Chapter 8

THE MORNING AFTER

I awoke exhausted, the third day since the incident at the station. I had gotten less than five hours of uninterrupted sleep since the murder investigation started, meaning five hours out of 48, and we hadn't gotten *anywhere* in moving forward with the investigation. It was simply going to suck. If we didn't get something that looked like a lead by the end of the day, Carol Whelan's murderer was going to go uncaught unless and until he committed another crime—*and* we could tie him back to the first murder.

The alarm got me and Jeremy and Mariel out of bed. With the usual sleep schedule of a child, Jeremy had rolled over and was still trying to sleep, even after I had showered, shaved and dressed for a new day. I took my rosary and left it tied around Jeremy's little hand, then I grabbed another one from the drawer. We kept all of those rosaries one gets in the mail and have them all blessed by whichever priest was on duty at Mass that Sunday...not much point to a rosary if it's not blessed.

I went into Jeremy's room to get a that print off of his sheets, perhaps bring it into the lab. If it was real blood, it should be black and crusty by now and would need to be delicately handled.

...Except it was gone. The hand print was never there. Even

though I saw it and photographed it the night before. I took out my phone. The image was gone from there, too.

I really hope I'm not losing my mind.

I started my walk even earlier than usual, since I had an errand to run ahead of time. As a Eucharistic Minister, I also served as an extraordinary minister of Holy Communion. My pyx was gilt, with a little silver Celtic cross design on the lid.

I modified my usual route to work. Instead of walking down Winchester, I turned left sooner and went down along the service road to the Cross Island Expressway. It was on the way to Saint Gregory the Great Church, through a nice neighborhood that could have easily been confused for suburban, if it weren't for the density. Each house had a nice little patch of grass, just to pretend that there was an option for floral customization. Each house had a slate roof and aluminum siding, with colors ranging from white to yellow to blue.

In short, it was a nice little neighborhood that could have served as the setting for an 80s sitcom, if the homes were a little bigger to accommodate the cast.

The house I ended up at was a pale mint green. I knocked, and the door opened immediately. The woman who answered was a home health aid. She was late middle-aged, black, with a lazy eye that was a little jaundiced. She wasn't a nurse, since there was nothing medically wrong with the patient aside from being old and unable to move from point A to point B without assistance.

"She in the living room," she said with a Caribbean accent so thick, I was expecting her to welcome me in the name of Baron Samedi—which would have been awkward on a number of levels.

I stepped inside. The smell was one part hospital, one part old people, and one part baby wipes and powder, in part because there were no windows open in the entire house.

The woman in question was Angela Darrin. I could still see that she had been pretty in her youth. But now she was in her mid-eighties, with a few wrinkles added for effect. Her hair was snow-white, and she was a little heavy-set.

"Hey, Angela."

Her eyes opened. They were pale and watery and didn't focus on me for a long minute. Her smile flickered a little. "Hello."

"Hi."

"Do I know you?"

I shook my head. "Naw. I only came down for a special delivery."

I reached into my coat pocket and pulled out the pyx, and her smile flickered again. I went through the rite and slipped her a wafer.

"She doesn't have long to live," the aide said on my way out the door. "This will do nothing."

I spared her a glance on my way out the door. "How do you figure?"

"She will still die."

I shrugged. "In which case, you have to wonder if you're in the wrong kind of work."

I left the house humming *Live and Let Die*, music from the decade when Roger Moore had played Bond.

The road to the station from there was down the service road, down to Braddock Avenue and making a right at the tank. (It was a Veterans of Foreign Wars hall, hence the decoration). I walked along, calm and collected about the odd experience with the home health aid. Who took such a job if they had that attitude?

My thoughts then drifted to Carol Whelan. There were only about two hundred murders a year in New York these days. It was a legacy left by one of the better mayors the city ever had. The policies laid down in the 1990s were so effective, not even the two mayors who followed could have screwed it up. The odds of one of those murders happening in a secure neighborhood, all day long, down the block from me, and that it was one of my son's friends...

Before the nightmare of last night, Jeremy had nearly been inconsolable. I was surprised he was able to get anything like sleep even before the little haunting began.

I didn't know what was going on, but I was going to enjoy throwing this one in jail. Yes, in jail. Because this was a murder case, not a *Lethal Weapon* movie.

I went up Braddock and was stopped cold when, a few blocks away from the station house I heard the booming chatter of automatic gunfire.

Unfortunately, one thing came to mind.

I broke into a run, handing a slight left around a school, which came out diagonally across the street from the station. An SUV had cut off the street, and two thugs fired at the station from behind the vehicle.

I came down at one knee behind a parked car, drew my gun, and watched them. They both wore jeans and hoodies, as though that was their definition of low-key. I was half a block away, watching each of the two men stop and reload once each.

After they reloaded, I stood and moved towards them. Neither one of them turned around. I closed to twenty or thirty feet, then opened fire. I didn't yell my identification, since they obviously didn't care about shooting police officers. I struck one of them in the back of the head. The gunfire was so loud, the other guy didn't notice that his partner was dead.

I closed, keeping my eye on the second shooter. He had emptied his gun again and pulled back, ready to reload, when I burst forward and clubbed him over the head with my pistol.

Two down. Though it would help to know how many more there are.

I peaked out around the SUV and saw that it was a nightmare. A few dozen men had surrounded the station at the front and the sides. Large SUVs were blocking the streets from both sides of 222nd street, and both of the side streets around the station. The entire building was under siege.

I looked back at the man I'd clubbed. He began to stir, and I curb-stomped him, hoping to keep him down this time. I kicked the weapons out of his grasp. I considered taking the weapon but that would be a last resort. Test-firing a weapon I've never seen before this moment was a really bad idea, and firing a gun I've never shot before was a recipe for disaster.

I flipped the unconscious gunman with my foot and winced. The shooter had extensive facial tattoos. The shooters were MS-13. They were there for Rene Ormeno.

The nearest police stations were miles away, each, and that was assuming that these people hadn't also sent kill squads to keep the other stations busy.

I was working out a plan of attack when the team of gunman directly in front of the station brought an RPG out of the back of their SUV.

Our Father, who art in Heaven, please help me save my men.

I drew down on the pair and fired. The first bullet struck the SUV in front of them and made them jump. One of them jumped out of cover, and a bullet from the station caught himin the chest. Another two struck him in the chest again, dropping him to the street.

Unfortunately, his cohort drew his hand gun and shot me in the chest.

Chapter 9

AFTER ACTION

When looking into declaring a person a Saint, one of the first things they do is disregard every miracle attributed to them while alive. Rome had made the same discovery about eyewitnesses that cops had—eyewitnesses were notoriously unreliable. The church prefers to assess miracles from a safe distance, with a lot of scientific tests in the way, and as much negative press to consider as possible. Heck, during the canonization process for Mother Teresa, the Church brought in notorious atheist Christopher Hitchens to give his list of complaints against her. Canonizations like the distance of time and attempt to be as objective as possible, if not directly adversarial: the official known as the devil's advocate had disappeared after Vat69 as the Catholic church-mice referred to the Vatican Council of half a century ago. Even if actions a person performed while alive were verified, proven miracles, that said nothing about the post-mortem state of their souls. Who knows what last minute thoughts as one lay dying could cause havoc to one's immortal soul?

In the particular instance, were the church to have examined the shootout at the 105th precinct, there would be nothing that couldn't be excused by ballistics.

The bullet fired at me was a nine-millimeter hardball. If you ever held one of those bullets, it would be about the size of an Aspirin, or a Tylenol tablet. It relied on the velocity of the bullet as a projectile to make it lethal. This is unlike a forty-five or thirty-eight caliber round, which are so much heavier, one could feel the difference by hefting the bullet. This difference is one of the many reasons that earlier nine-millimeters have been looked down upon. Many lacked penetration power...later versions *over*penetrated, passing through a target and not really stopping them.

And this isn't even accounting for the various and sundry things that can go wrong with bullets in the process from being manufactured, through storage, up until the point that the firing pin strikes the blasting cap. In short, a lot of things can go wrong at a lot of steps between the bullet being made to the time it's fired.

So, when the round struck me in the chest, and dropped me down to the street, there was a long moment where I was certainly dead. The point of impact was in my heart. The bastard had some great aim.

The first thing I did when I could move again was smack my chest where the bullet struck.

My hand landed on the pyx I carried for my home visit that morning. I took it out of the pocket and looked at it.

The pyx, filled with blessed wafers, had caught the bullet. *The Lord is my rock and my fortress and my deliverer, in whom I take refuse, my shield...though I never expected You would act quite so literally. Blessed be the name of the Lord.*

I sat up, gun ready, and stood.

The man who shot me had picked up the RPG and was leveling it at the station. The gunfire had intensified on both sides, with my people trying to keep the RPG from entering into play, and the MS-13 gunman trying to suppress the police.

I leaned up against the SUV and used the hood as a shooting platform, taking careful aim at the MS-13 thug with the RPG.

Hail Mary, full of Grace, the Lord—

I fired.

I missed.

My bullet did not strike the attacker. It did not touch him. It struck over a foot away from my target.

It struck along the barrel of the RPG The launcher jerked at a sixty-degree angle as it fired. I dropped flat as the insanely long stream of fire came out if the back end, torching three of the MS-13 gunman coming to back him up. The grenade struck the second car blocking 222nd street, between the first car and the cars blocking the side road. The resulting explosion took out all four cars, and everyone behind them.

I blinked. *Wow. Now that's what I call a miracle.*

I wheeled around, circling around the back of the SUV, heading for the remaining MS-13 gunmen. The few that remained were confused by the sudden turn around. There were four SUV's intact, and there could have been as many as sixteen remaining, easy.

I swapped out magazines, loading in a fresh one, giving me fifteen and one in the chamber. I had a second full one, and a partial.

I took a deep breath to calm myself, and swung around the back of the SUV.

I moved towards the grill of the first SUV blocking 222nd street. One of the gunman spotted me and raised his automatic weapon, one-handed, held at a ninety-degree, "gangsta style."

I fired three times, all three in the chest. *Deliver me from my enemies, my God—*

I leaned to the side, at an angle, pushing my gun forward. "Freeze!"

Deliver me from those who work evil—

The gunman couldn't decide if he was running away from me or shooting at me. He ended up in a sideways jog, while trying to fire across his body with a gun that looked like a Mac-10.

Save me from bloodthirsty men. I fired three more times, punching into his ribs and arm. He fell down, sprawled on the sidewalk. Behind him was a gunman who was far more certain about what he was going to do, and had taken up a two-handed firing position.

I hit the ground. *They lie in wait for my life, and stir up strife against me.* I fired another burst, tearing through his knee, gun, and throat.

I heard a scrape of gravel behind me, rolled onto my back, and fired straight into the chest of another gang banger. The bullets caught him at only a few feet, and he was knocked back off his feet. *Spare none who treacherously plot evil.*

I rolled back and fired three rounds at the next attacker, charging around the SUVs. They caught up, and he went straight down.

I ejected the magazine and slammed a new one in. There was still a round in the chamber.

But I will sing of Your strength. I will sing aloud of Your steadfast love in the morning. For You have been to me a fortress, and a refuge in the day of my distress...And did I get all of them already?

"Police!"

"Freeze!"

"Drop the weapon!"

I let myself relax. The rest of the gunmen must have been hiding or on the run.

"Free—Oh, hi, Tom."

I stared up at my partner. Alex Packard holstered his gun. "You been lying around on the job the whole time? We've had some excitement here we could have used you for."

I arched a brow at him. "Really? You're going to be like that?"

Packard smiled and shrugged before reaching down. I took the offered hand and made it to my feet. He looked around, truly appreciating the devastation, and gave a low whistle.

"Hell of a party," he said.

I laughed humorlessly. "You could say that."

"Yeah...hey, what was the gag on that text last night?"

I blinked hard so I could clear my head. "Gag? What do you mean?"

"Last night, you sent me a photo of a bloody hand print on a white background. This morning, the photo is just a white sheet. What is it, some sort of self-deleting thing? A virus for the phone? What?"

It took me a moment to remember that I had texted him a photograph of Carol Whelan's bloody hand print from my son's room last night. "It wiped itself from your phone, too?"

"You bet it did. What's going on?"

"No idea. Wish I knew." I shook my head. "Later, I'm going to tell you about last night."

As we walked back towards the station as other people cleaned up the mess, I noted the arsenal that had been brought to bear in this little jailbreak attempt. Some of them were armed with professional weapons: AUG Steyrs, Igrams, and a scattering of M4s. But half of them were armed with home-made automatic weapons, made in a metalworking shop. Some of them even fired shotgun shells on full auto. If a cop ever tells you he thinks gun laws are stupid, it's probably because he's run into a shootout like this.

We got inside, stepped over the shell casings, and around the glass. This was going to be a nightmare for the janitorial staff, no matter how they sliced this one. We made our way to our desk and hoped that we would be allowed out again sometime soon.

And I stopped in my tracks. There was that freaking smell again. From Hayes, and the crime scene, and even a little from Rene Ormeno.

I look over at our desk. It was far away from the shooting, at the back of the bullpen, and apparently untouched. On top of it was a cardboard box, like you'd get in the mail, and closed with packing tape. Next to it was a bottle with a tag wrapped around it.

"Someone get you a present?" Packard asked, moving towards the bottle.

"Don't touch it," I ordered. "Glove up."

I crouched down and looked carefully at the bottle, and my gut dropped out. I breathed out a slight sigh of relief that it probably wasn't a bomb. "Get some of our science geeks up here," I told Packard. "We're going to need them."

"I'm sure they're coming up here already. Why do you ask?"

I nodded at the wine bottle while I slipped a glove onto my left hand. "It's a bottle of Chianti."

"So?"

"Didn't you tell me that Carol Whelan's liver was missing? We read *Silence of the Lambs*."

Packard blinked, then grimaced. "Ugh. You must be kidding."

"I'm just going to assume that there are some fava beans in the box as well." I reached forward with my gloved hand, and slightly opened the card, wrapped around the neck of the wine bottle.

The message was only two words: From Hell.

Chapter 10

FORENSICS

After an officer-involved shooting, it is standard operating procedure that those cops involved be put on modified assignment, and they ride a desk until it's cleared up. Even if the shooting is good, IA investigates.

However, if that was going to be the case here, most of the station was going to be off the street for the next week. And in this case, it was a fairly clear case of an attempted breakout by MS-13. And considering that I was the one that pulled the trigger on the bodies in the street, I was going to be the number-one priority. Technically, I would be riding a desk until next week and turn in my gun. But I had a homicide of a little girl to investigate, and Packard had a gun. As I told my CO: "If there's any trouble, Alex will shoot them."

Packard didn't laugh.

The first order of business was to call Mariel and tell her that I was safe and sound and not to worry about a shootout at the station. I wasn't even scratched.

The second piece of business was to tell Packard that our victim was my son's friend in school.

His response was to shrug. "You didn't know at the time, and you've never met her. Her parents didn't recognize you. Can you think of any new lines of inquiry we have now? No? Then let's get going."

At ten, we made it to the Medical Examiner. First, we had to pass a dozen assistants who looked green and physically ill. I assumed that they had all joined in on the examination of the corpse of Carol Whelan.

The professional we needed was Doctor Sinead Holland. She was a pretty brunette with a heart-shaped face, a smile on her lips, and brown eyes that always caught the light. Her background was Northern European, up near Norway, giving her high cheekbones, and eyes that were nearly Asiatic.

Today, though, she was a little less bouncy.

Carol Whelan was covered with a sheet on a slab, and Doctor Holland stayed up against a wall, on the other end of the room.

We walked in and said nothing, and she looked up from the clipboard to look at us. "You two have this bad tendency lately to bring me some really nasty stuff, you know that, right?"

"We didn't generate it," Packard answered. "We just caught it. We'd rather give it to someone else. Like the flu."

Holland rolled her eyes but gave a slight smile. It faded again as she pointed to the sheet with her pen. "What do you know about what happened to little Carol Whelan?"

"Really bad things," Packard answered.

She frowned. If she had been hoping that we would fill in statements for her, she had another think coming. "The disarticulation of the joints exhibits some surgical skill, but also hacked apart, by someone with a hacksaw, a hammer, something like that. Half the bones aren't so much cut as crushed, like he broke them with a hammer. That was perimortem. *Most* of what you can see was perimortem."

I didn't throw up my breakfast, even though that meant that Whelan was alive during all of that.

Packard nodded. "This we saw. What did we miss?"

Holland didn't say anything but handed us a series of pictures. They were extreme closeups, so we didn't get the full picture—except that these were images carved on skin. "Those are all over her body. And I mean all over. You couldn't see them under all the blood."

I studied them, even though I knew the source. Holland had made this as painless as possible, given the circumstances. "Any idea what they mean?"

"Not a clue."

"At least, now we know what he was doing for eight hours," Packard said. "This had to take time, even if she were dead first."

Holland shook her head. "Not done yet. Your pervert left behind some DNA, in all of the usual places, as well as whatever was handy."

Packard flinched this time. We didn't need to ask; we could put those pieces together.

"What else?" I asked. There had to be more.

"Your box from the station? There was nothing forensically inter-esting on the outside, but you were right about the contents. It was pate."

I gagged this time. I closed my eyes, said a quick prayer, and opened them.

She continued: "It was also human and *half* the weight of what I would expect the liver of a girl her age would be."

Packard gave me a look. "Considering the Hannibal the Cannibal joke he delivered, I'm going to speculate that we already know where the rest of the liver went."

"That's your job," Holland said. She sighed, and she sounded relieved, like this was almost over. "Also, you know the liver was removed, but from what I could put together, there's also a significant amount of tissue missing, as well as the heart."

"The *heart*?" Packard and I exclaimed at once.

She nodded. "Looks like he reached under the rib cage and extracted it that way."

He looked at me. "Can you even eat a human heart?"

"I try not to ask such questions," I told him. I looked back to Holland. "You know, I've heard everything but cause of death. You have one?"

"I have four. The blood loss, or just removal of the heart, the liver or ... oh, yeah. That's that last part. Did you catch the hole in her head?"

I nodded. "In the crown. Large bore needle, easily. Possibly something even bigger."

"Yeah. That's probably what removed the other part."

Packard groaned. "Another? Which one *now*?"

"Her brain. It looked like someone jammed a needle in and sucked her brains out."

Packard rolled his eyes. "He has liver pate, maybe he wants to make sweet breads, too."

Holland sighed, and laid down the clipboard. "You've probably already checked, but I added the additional details to both a VICAP search, as well as the profile you sent to Freeman. Nothing on VICAP, though I have to tell you, I this feels familiar."

"A case you've worked on?" I asked.

Holland shook her head. "Can't put my finger on it." She shook her head, dismissing the thought for now. "Do me a favor guys? Get this son of a bitch."

"Deal."

Chapter 11

BANKRUPT

C reedmoor Mental Hospital, or as I like to call it, the nut house, was a sprawling 200-acre campus with a large, looming building in the center. Part of the Soviet school of manufacturing, the main building was a beige concrete bunker nearly twenty stories high. Like much of the area around Queens Village, it used to be part of farmland, in this case owned by the Creed family. It became a firing range for the National Guard and the NRA in the late 1800s. In 1892, the land went back to the state, mostly due to declining public interest and mounting noise complaints from the growing neighborhood.

The first hospital opened there in 1912, the "Farm Colony of Brooklyn State Hospital" at Creedmoor—because it was a way to send urban psychiatric patients to rural fresh air. The move to deinstitutionalize had shrunk the campus, turning one part into the Queens County Farm Museum. Another became the Queens Children's Psychiatric Center, as well as a public school and a teaching school.

I arrived there at noon, driving up to the main entrance off of Winchester. Packard had left me the car and did his own work. The main thing was that this was a job I could do without needing a firearm. I shouldn't technically get into a firefight at either the Medical Examiner's or while talking to the consulting shrink.

In the case of my expert police profiler and psychologist, he was in the big ugly building. He was a police counselor, as well as many other things.

He was Father Richard Freeman, Order of Preachers, a first order Dominican priest. Of course he was a Dominican, when you want a truly *educated* Catholic, you don't go to the Pseudo-intellectuals in the Jesuits.

Freeman was in his late forties, skinny, with just enough gray at his temples to make him an interesting stunt double for a comic book scientist. He wore his black shirt and white collar with a lab coat over it. He was a bit nebbishy, but what would you expect from someone with three PhDs? In German, he would have been addressed as doctor doctor doctor Freeman.

Freeman came to meet me at the front door, trying to make the creepy mental hospital more welcoming than the setting of a horror movie. "I would ask how you're doing, but I've seen the murder book. Come up."

Freeman's office was a walk-in closet, only packed with a desk, three file cabinets, a bookcase, and a chair. Even the desk had little room, with a monstrous late-80s computer and monitor on it. The shelves were filled with books and papers, both religious and psychological. He only had two crosses on the shelves, though that was more than I would expect—the psychological profession was not exactly kind to Father Freeman's real day job. Both chairs—his and the one for his guest—were wooden, rickety, and hard to get comfortable in. If he was unhappy with the setup, he didn't show it.

Then again, there were a lot of people who referred to his office as "the OP Center," because it made the Order of Preachers sound so military.

He leaned back in his chair and folded his hands over his chest. "I'm not sure what I can tell you that you don't already know. You don't need me to tell you that you have a sadistic psychopath out there."

I smiled. "True enough."

"Based on dis-articulation, I concur with Doctor Holland about the killer having medical training." He reached forward and pulled a file out of the drawer. From the file, he pulled three photos.

"Do you know what these are?"

"A cow, a strange triangle, and an apple being offered up to a circle?"

Freeman shook his head. He tapped the cow. "Moloch, Carthaginian deity of money and demon. Standard form of worship was for the population to give over their biggest drain on their wallets and send them into the fire pits."

"I'm guessing it wasn't their lawyers."

"Their children."

I winced. "Child sacrifice. Nice." I frowned at the photo. So our killer was also a bad artist, on top of everything else. "At least, it fits. The triangle with the lines and the oval?"

"Ever hear of Aleister Crowley?"

"Him I've heard of. Some sort of Satanist?"

"More or less. He was one part occultist and one part cult leader." He took the photo of the triangle, and, with a pencil, traced a perimeter around the lines shooting forth from the triangle, connecting the tips. The lines radiating from the triangle formed a six-pointed star around the triangle. He added a dot to oval in the middle of the triangle. It was an eye in the middle.

"This," Freeman told me, "is one of Crowley's symbols. It doesn't match Moloch, but Crowley was already into summoning demons."

To say that I had a bad feeling about this would be to drastically, even catastrophically, underestimate the sense that everything was going to Hell in a hand-basket. "What about the last one? The circle with lines and the apple?"

"I had this printed this morning from a computer that is a little more this-decade than the parish computer. Hopefully, no one will ask any questions." He grabbed the second drawer and gave it a good yank ... then did it again, until it popped open. He pulled out a photo that he had covered with several post-it notes. The part that wasn't covered looked exactly like what I had seen at the crime scene. Only the circle with lines from it was the sun. The apple was gripped in someone's hand. The rest of the arm was underneath all the notes.

"Can I see what the prize behind door number 1 is?" I asked, my finger sliding under the post-its, but not lifting. Freeman nodded soberly.

"Oh crap."

The apple wasn't an apple. It was a heart. I could tell mostly because the person it had been ripped out of was on a little pyramid, held down by four other people, while the fifth held the heart aloft.

"Aztec," I murmured. "Has to be Aztec. Rip someone's heart out to keep the sun moving. Also, the art style looks Meso-American." I cast my mind back to half-remembered anecdotes. "They didn't just cut the heart out though, right, Father? They wrapped it in a package of the victim's own flesh."

Freeman nodded. "When I saw the ME report about the missing skin, it sent me on the trail."

"At least that explains the heart."

He took photos from the file, the photos of the carvings in Carol Whelan's skin, and spread them on the desk like a deck of cards. "All of these images are Satanic or demonic in origin, Tom. These are genuine symbols, not some idiot who picked up random images symbols from a Dan Brown novel. This isn't some nut playing at Satanism. These symbols are old and ancient, going back thousands of years. Some of them I had to work fairly hard to dig up."

I closed my eyes, leaned back, and banged my head against the wall behind me a few times. "Great. Just great." Sigh. "A dead little girl—that my son knows, by the way—is murdered, and everything just starts going straight down to Hell, and I think I'm losing my mind on top of that. I—"

My cell phone rang, loud and obnoxiously. It was Darth Vader's theme, the ring I gave my mother-in-law. I groaned, grabbed it, and put it on speaker, just so Father Freeman could get an idea of what I put up with on a regular basis.

"Hello, Martha, how are you doing?" I asked.

There was nothing from the phone but static. I growled, then turned off the phone entirely. "Not to mention that I need a new phone plan."

Freeman gave me a curious look. He was leaning in, his dark, piercing eyes studying me like I was a new insect. "Tell me about it?"

"What's to tell?" I held up the phone before slipping it away. "Ever since I got this case, my phone doesn't work. I don't sleep. I'm hearing things, seeing things, and smelling things. If I can feel or taste phantom sensations, I'll be five for five senses."

Freeman said nothing for a long moment. When I didn't add anything, he waved his finger in a rolling motion, that I should continue. I shrugged. "I had this guy at the station two days ago, in the morning. Hayes. He smelled like decomp, only worse. Hayes went after me; he ripped up the station, single-handed, trashed all of the windows, seemingly by screaming, and suicided in his cell after he's thrown in. No one else could smell him, and no one else could smell his scent at various places, too."

Freeman arched a brow. "Such as where? The station and...?"

"At the crime scene, which is stupid, because I know he's dead. I even caught a whiff of something similar on an MS-13 perp I busted early yesterday morning. And then in my *house*."

Freeman's eyes widened at that part and held up a hand. "Go back to the gang banger. Would you say that he could be classified as evil?"

I stared at him for a long moment and gave a sharp laugh. "You're kidding? All of them are, and they're not very subtle about it. But yeah, he's a pretty evil son of a bitch. Did you have something in mind?"

"Not quite yet, but tell me, did you have anything strange happen before Hayes and the station?"

"You could say that. I caught a purse snatcher." I frowned, and waggled my head back and forth a bit, weighing the scales of telling a shrink and a priest about an incident that I was now starting to worry about. "I somehow got ahead of him. And I mean one moment I was chasing him, and another moment, I was in front of him. But somehow, for some reason, I was also behind him, still running to catch up, and I could see myself in front of the runner, clothes-lining him."

Freeman's eyebrows went up, but his lips went down. He was confused. But I couldn't blame him. So was I. "I'm starting to think I have brain damage."

Freeman cocked his head, his face resetting. "How do you figure? Does it have to do with your inability to sleep? Or the two places at once incident?"

"Actually, the sleep problem is a separate issue. There might be some sort of gas leak in the house, because all three of us felt it."

Freeman encouraged me to go on, and I did, explaining everything that happened during the night, from the phone, to the footsteps in the attic, Jeremy's nightmare vision and the hand print that went with it, the shape at the foot of the bed, and how it just suddenly stopped.

"Jeremy must have been upset," Freeman prompted.

"No kidding. He was scared out of his mind. We started saying the rosary, he calmed down. Thankfully, there was nothing else after that. Thank God."

"Indeed." Father Freeman leaned back, took a slow breath, and said, "I think I have a solution."

I perked up and leaned forward. "To which part? The Whelan murder, or my going crazy?"

"Both. For your problems, there could be an explanation for everything. You could have just experienced multiple hallucinations. You could have blacked out during the chase, and everything you think you saw is cause for an MRI. This smell you caught on Hayes, at the crime scene, and on the MS-13 thug could be a genetic quirk."

I raised a brow, incredulous. "A quirk? Such as?"

Freeman shrugged, spreading his hands wide. "There are people who can taste a flavor to litmus paper. It's a paper that tests for acids and bases in chemistry. Some people can lick it and taste a flavor to it, and some can't. It's a genetic quirk. Perhaps you can smell things others can't because of that."

"And last night? The phone calls?"

"As you say," he answered casually, "one could be a gas leak, and the other could be a cruddy phone plan."

"Uh huh." I stared at him for a long moment, studying him. His face was perfectly placid and relaxed. He was a poker player who didn't want to signal his tells. "And what's the other version?"

"The other version fits together better, but I don't think you're going to want to hear any of it."

"Try me."

Freeman pursed his lips in thought, considering how to begin. I'd seen him do it a lot, and I knew what it meant. I couldn't quite read him like a book, but still. "What do you know of the supernatural abilities of saints who were wonder workers?"

I shrugged, and rattled off a few. "Joe Cupertino could fly. Thomas Aquinas levitated at the Eucharist. Padre Pio could read minds in the confessional. There's the stigmata. There's Saint Francis talking down a wolf. So, yeah, I know a few of them. Why?"

Freeman shrugged, as though he were just having an offhand thought. "These powers and abilities of people who would later be canonized also include bilocation, as well as the ability to smell evil."

I stopped for a moment. But stopping, my mind and my face were as the blue screen of death. *Is he saying what I think he's saying.* "So are you saying—"

Freeman held up his hands, as though keeping them clean of a mess. "I'm not saying anything. But, for the moment, let's suggest that you were, to some degree, developing the supernatural abilities that one might find in a saint—"

I held up a hand. "But we're not, right?"

"No. But if we were, we have a hint of a motive." Father Freeman slipped his hand into the file again, and pulled out another photo. It was a photo of the back of Carol Whelan's closet, saying that the Patron Saint of Detectives should come and get him.

"Yeah, I didn't get that. We have a patron saint of police, not detectives."

Freeman smiled, and looked at me like I was slow, which I was. "He was talking about you."

Chapter 12

DEMONS IN THE ATTIC

"Would you like me to list the ways in which I am not a saint?" Freeman's smile was one of his patient ones, that he used for the slow children, and the slower adults. "I didn't say you were. I just mean that he was *calling* you a saint. He's taunting you."

I shook my head and sighed. After a hesitation, I said, "Okay. Fine. He thinks I'm some sort of saint. What do you think?"

"I think you've some abilities like unto a saint. I think you can bilocate, as you did a couple of mornings ago, and you can smell evil, which you've been doing since the start of your trials."

I leaned back in the chair. I wasn't dismissive of the abilities of the saints. I knew plenty of them, and I wasn't going to disregard any out of hand. My problem was with ... well, me, being a saint. Who would make me a saint? Or consider me saintly? That was the hard part to swallow.

I tried to follow the line of reasoning. The only way someone could taunt me with being a Saint of Anything would be for said someone to know I had these abilities. But since I didn't know I had these abilities, this left someone else ... or some*thing* else.

I frowned, not that I was considering the prospect ludicrous, but because I was taking it seriously. If the smell of Hayes was the smell of evil, Hayes had known I could smell it on him.

Though assuming that Hayes knew I was able to smell the evil on him, that's quite a leap for anyone to take. But it also assumes that he ... knew he was evil? How does that even work? Unless ...

I groaned. Again, because I took the prospect seriously. "I'm hoping you're not going to suggest that this is a demon?"

"Because it's impossible?"

I scoffed. "No. Have you considered how exactly I arrest someone possessed by a *demon*? Or worse: prosecute? And what is the motive here? He's a demon, it's what he does?"

Freeman gave a surprised laugh, either that I was treating it seriously, or at the absurdity of the idea of prosecution. "Considering the number of jokes with lawyers in Hell, I can see how it would be a problem," he drolled. "And given that the toxicology on Hayes came back negative—yes, I checked—I can't see how he pulled off the battle with you and the station the other day. As to your other question, there is motive: it knows what you are, or what you could be. He wants to crush you."

I nodded slowly, connecting the dots. Hayes was the host body for the demon the day before yesterday. When Hayes committed suicide —or the demon drove him to it—the demon was free to move on to a new host. The demon decided that it was going to come after me by attacking my family, starting with one of Jeremy's only friends.

Which meant that brutally torturing and murdering little Carol Whelan was to get at me. And for what? Because I had the audacity to pray? Go to church? Try not to suck at being a human being?

I took a breath. I said a quick prayer in my head to calm down and think about this rationally. If a demon was coming after me, then...

"So what was last night?" I asked. "The demon jerking me around?"

Freeman nodded. "It sounds like demonic infestation, straight out of the playbook. And you said it stopped when you started the rosary. Even the phone calls sound like harassment. I'm going to guess it's a nightly practice, if it's not already."

That actually hurt a bit. "It usually is, when I get home on time." It was one of the perks of my job: lousy pay and any free time with your family is a theoretical concept. "What's next? Heck, how would that take us with the profile? We still have to catch this sucker. I don't care if he's from Hell or Hoboken. We still have to stop him."

Freeman nodded and leaned forward. "Part of it will be simple: the demon's host isn't going to be something or someone like an innocent victim. This host was already open and ready not only to possession, but to kill. Given the level of violence I see here, if the host doesn't have his own experience in this area, I'll be surprised. Unlike *The Exorcist,* no one goes from innocent little girl to ravaging demon so easily."

I nodded slowly and leaned back in the chair. I had actually read the book for *The Exorcist,* and that had a heavily-detailed explanation on possession as well as the tests the Church used to verify it. It was based off of a real case of possession. The little boy involved (not a girl) had this bad habit of playing with things like Oujia boards, seances, etc. Demons need a way in and will take any opening that they can get.

In short, do not play with demonic things, and demonic things do not play with you.

There wasn't a lot to go by. There were no fingerprints. If the demon was smart enough to obscure his fingerprints but had let the human host leave his DNA at the crime scene, it was unlikely that the host was in the criminal system.

But if the host was ready to kill like this, then the possessed had to have been fairly active already. If the possessed hadn't already been a killer, then this was a hell of a lot of escalation. That was unlikely at best. And again, the host had to be open to becoming this big a monster in the first place.

Which means that the host, all by himself, was probably this big a monster even before the demon got its hands on him. But if he wasn't in the system, he was smart enough to not get caught in the first place.

This was going to be so much trouble, it wasn't even funny.

"What about the photograph I took of the bloody hand print?"

"People around Padre Pio insisted that the devil screwed up his papers and records."

I grimaced. If that was the case, the this was going to be even worse. Police work thrived on paperwork. If a demon could corrupt hard copies and computer copies of everything from my DD5s to the evidence logs and tags, then prosecuting this case could become impossible.

I sighed. "Is there anything else I can do for you?"

"Not right now. I'm not even sure how much of what I've said will help you to find him. I fear that it is more likely that he will find you."

I nodded as I rose. "Concur. If all this is because it thinks it found a saint to torment, and I'm it? I have no doubt it's going to continue to come after me and mine."

We shook hands. "You want me to walk you down?"

I was about to decline, but I considered the conversation I just had and that I was still alone in a mental hospital. If that didn't sound like a bad end in a horror movie, I didn't know what did.

"Sure, I can always use the company."

Freeman smiled, as though he could read my thoughts on the matter. But I wasn't going to be embarrassed. Frankly, being scared out of my mind wouldn't be out of line.

As we walked out, the priest asked, "You worried?"

"Scared outta my mind," I admitted.

He smiled. "Good. I'd worry if you weren't. How is Jeremy doing with his friend's death?"

"Honestly? I can't tell. I wasn't there when he got the news. Last night. I spent most of my time keeping him calm or securing the house. And this morning, I had to deliver Communion, so I left before he even woke up."

Freeman said nothing as we went out to the parking lot. Then again, he didn't have to.

"Perhaps I can manage the bilocation to spend time at home and work the job at the same time," I suggested.

He laughed. "It wouldn't be the worst use that I've heard about."

As I caught sight of the car, I stopped and caught Father Freeman before he kept going. There was a brown cardboard box on the hood of my unmarked car.

"Since I don't trust my phone," I said, calmly and quietly, "could you go back inside and call 911, use my name and badge number, and ask them to send the bomb squad?"

Freeman nodded hurriedly and ran back inside.

I moved forward. Considering the last package that I had delivered from this psycho, I wasn't going to lay money on what was in it. It could be more organs or it could be a full-fledged bomb. I wasn't going to take any chances.

Then I caught the smell again.

I whirled around, reaching for the gun that wasn't there and ended up with a knife in my guts.

After all, you can't become a saint until you're dead.

Chapter 13

BECOMING A SAINT

The thing that stabbed me wasn't human. While it had the shape of a human in the same way that a chalk outline did, it was a black mass that seemed to flicker back and forth, like I had just been stabbed by a mass of dark static.

Okay, I'm willing to entertain the possibility of a demonic murderer.

I grabbed for the wrist of what stabbed me and held on, hoping to lock it in place as I elbowed my assailant in the face. The elbow is one of the hardest bones in the human body. Consequently, elbow strikes hurt like hell.

Bringing my hand back the other way, I clapped my hand down on the shoulder and drove my knee into its groin and its stomach.

It didn't stagger or even really react to anything I did to it. It flicked its arm and threw me against the windshield of car parked in the lot.

I groaned. It was less than pleasant.

The shape came for me, scalpel held high. I kicked out with one leg on the hood of the car, twisting my body, so the scalpel came down on the hood of the car instead of my head. Instead of grabbing for the weapon, I hammered my fist down on the butt of the scalpel, driving it into the hood of the car, snapping the blade. I reared back with my other foot and kicked the shape in the head—or at least where the head should be.

The figure took a step back but not much farther than that.

I scrambled back, off the hood, and landed on the other side of the car. I was at least going to be able to keep a car between me and it, right?

Then the car between us flipped into the air, coming straight for my face.

I dropped flat and hit the ground just in time. The dark shape hadn't even touched the vehicle. It just flew through the air to take my hair off.

It took several steps towards me, and I rolled out of the way and onto my feet.

It closed, moving with unearthly speed. I hunkered down, almost in a wrestler's crouch, arms wide open, ready to grapple. I was vulnerable, in a prime position to get kicked in the face.

The creature raised a knee, ready to kick out, and take my head clean off.

It fell for the trap.

I ducked as the kick came straight for my face. Once it was over my shoulder, I sprang up, wrapping my arms around the leg and drove straight into the killer. I had it on its back, and I could feel an ankle underneath the flickering, amorphous illusion over it. I stomped down between the killer's legs to pin him in place as I jerked the ankle around. I did my best to twist the leg off.

It laughed, like the sound of a thousand razor blades clacking.

Uh oh.

The leg I held reared back, and I leaped off to the side to avoid the coming kick. The killer was on its feet in an eye-blink. And it had two scalpels this time.

Then it spoke. It sounded like the growl of an angry dog the size of an Abrams tank.

"I knew what you were when you smelled me that morning." It stepped forward, brandishing the scalpels with a flourish. "I will break you, ruin you, crush you. Destroy your faith, your life, and wreck you utterly."

I burst backwards right before it jabbed at the air in front of me. We circled each other, and it continued. "When we first met, I wasn't prepared for you. My host had grown weak. He was a husk I was nearly done with. But now, I'm prepared for you, Saint. And I will end you."

It swiped at me with one scalpel, then the other I didn't even bother ducking or weaving. I hurled my body out of the way and rolled. When I came to my feet, I still had my overcoat slashed in five places.

"I will kill your family," it boasted and kicked for my chest. I sidestepped, and it kicked out a window of a car behind me. It whirled and slashed, this time taking my sleeve, cutting my forearm and part of my jacket. "I will destroy everyone you know and love."

I reached into my pocket and took two things. The first was my car keys. Then I flicked open my key chain, which was a nice, 18-inch tactical baton. I palmed the second object into my left hand.

The shape laughed. "You think you can battle *me*? I saw the creation of your *universe*, and you think you can stop *me!*"

I smiled. "God, no."

Then I popped the cover on the pyx and threw it at the demon.

It screamed. The noise was somewhere between the Nazgul, the Shadows, nails on a blackboard, the squealing of brakes coming to a sudden stop, and pigs being tortured.

It leaped away, and the black static started to fade, revealing a man in a balaclava. The demon was taking no chances with the host this time. It was also smarter than I thought it was and nowhere near as arrogant.

He ran. I pursued. He headed straight for the exit, and I was hot on his heels. There was going to be nothing that would stop me from laying hands on this bastard...

Except a random idiot who pulled his car out of a parking slot and hit me with his car. I bounced off of the trunk, then the concrete. That was embarrassing.

Then I heard the sounds of sirens in the distance.

Now they show up.

The first person to stand over me wasn't even the idiot who hit me —he worked his car around me and drove off, the schmuck—but Alex Packard, my partner.

"Lying down on the job again?" he drolled. He looked me over and saw my slashed up coat. He reached down and grabbed my arm, helping me to my feet. "Geez, Tommy, what butcher shop did you end up in?"

I leaned up against the trunk of another car. Nothing felt broken, but my body hated that I was even upright. "The killer was here." I pointed towards the exit. "About medium height. Maybe on the shorter side. Ski mask, brown leather jacket, black pants. He was just here, about a minute ago."

Packard looked me over, and noticed the one knife mark that wasn't a slash but a stab. "How did you survive a gut shot, Tommy?"

That was a good question, one that I hadn't even considered. Between the adrenaline and the car flipping over, it hadn't even entered my mind. I reached down and grabbed the park of my overcoat where I'd been stabbed the first time...

He had stabbed a little prayer book I kept on me at all times.

Okay. Maybe this saint thing isn't as stupid as I thought.

This day wasn't my day to die.

"Let's get you some aspirin and have someone here look you over. There has to be some real doctors in a place like this."

"You'd hope."

The bomb squad figured out relatively quickly that the box did not have a bomb. And I was right. I had suspected that the next organ we would get would be a heart, and parts would be missing, and that it would be from Carol Whelan.

I was right.

The box had a human heart in it. The heart was missing bites out of it, and the marks were made by human teeth. I was right about everything ... except that the heart was from an adult.

Chapter 14

EAT YOUR HEART OUT

I didn't take long to figure out where the adult heart had come from. Shortly after I had gotten changed at the station, a new call had come in with a fresh murder. They knew to call for me and Packard because the corpse was in a similar state of disarray as last time, only this time, it was spread out all over the yard. No one had noticed, because they just assumed that the victim was just setting up early for Halloween—the victim was "odd" to the accounts of all the neighbors and would do stuff like that.

They only started to note something was wrong when flies started to gather.

I didn't need anything more than that to realize who had been murdered. Not the name, not the address. I knew exactly where we were going to go.

I just didn't know how to tell my wife that one of her best friends was now one of my victims.

I told Packard about our victim, Erin Quintanilla, the perky goth who had only been over at my house the night we caught the Carol Whelan murder. I had just seen her under 48 hours ago.

"Think anyone is going to care about that?" I asked Packard as we headed for the car.

He shrugged. "Maybe. But you're already working the case. You're already involved. I can't see how replacing you at this point is going to be a help."

I frowned, and he laughed at me, taking over the driving.

It didn't take that long to get to Erin's house—a right out the front door and then a right four blocks down. We could have walked. It was a corner home built like a fort: the outside gate was a chain link fence that ran the length of the property, around the corner and to the garage in the back. The back yard was cordoned off with a taller, wooden fence. It was a nice home with plenty of lawn space, so it was very easy to go from the front gate to the front door without having to step over any body parts.

And I smelled the crime scene before I saw it. If this was the scent of evil, then it was growing stronger. I couldn't even smell the blood or decomp.

As Packard looked over the body parts strewn over the yard, he took it in. "For the record, I hate this case."

"You're not the only one."

It got stranger once we were in the house.

The inside of the house was surprisingly narrow, despite all of the yard space. It was not especially well lit. It was more for atmosphere than anything else. Then we found her "toy room." Starting with her Oujia board, straight from Toys R Us ("Age range 8 years old and up!" Packard snarked. "Must be 8 years old to summon Satan."). This led to her Saint candle collection ("Perfect for all your Santeria needs"). We won't even go into another room where she had a butcher's block for chickens, goats, and a few other animal parts I couldn't identify ("Presumably not for just having really fresh food").

"You know," I stated, "I knew she was into some strange stuff, but this? Not so much."

Packard scoffed, amused. "You mean that she didn't bring up how to butcher your own animals over Thanksgiving dinner?"

"She said it was..." I tried to consider what she had said the last time I had asked her about faith. "She said she practiced 'harmless rituals in order to deepen her spirituality.' I just thought that she meant she meditated and took long walks on the beach."

"Not quite."

I looked over the miscellaneous knickknacks Erin had owned. There were crystals of all shapes and sizes, from the small necklaces to the ten-pound crystals that formed within rocks. The whole room was a menagerie of spiritual confusion—everything from stacks of tarot cards wrapped in various colored silks to a collection of jars with twisted roots in human shapes. There was a mummified blue-bird in a lucite box, and enough crystals and strange looking stones to impress the gemologists at the Museum of Natural History. She had a potted dead tree with wood like bone sitting in one corner, with colored bottles over each branch. In another corner, she had stacked enough miscellaneous novena candles to light St Peter's Cathedral for a year stacked in one corner. Dream catchers and strands of fake flowers laced the windows. Various pagan figurines from a dozen pantheons dotted the room, each with its attendant shrine. One or two of them looked like they were in the process of being dismantled. The large densely packed bookshelf in the back was all over the map —everything from *The Key of Solomon the King*, to *How to be a Shaman in 30 Days*, something called *Goetia*, to anthropological texts about remote tribes in wild places, to a little subsection on feminist Wicca. She didn't just visit the metaphysical bookstore—she could have easily stocked one.

I didn't want to think about the interesting times that Forensics was going to have ahead of them.

I considered how the demon had gotten in. Yes, I was thinking of this guy as a straight up demon. But then again, as noted earlier, when someone was open to anything, any thing can wander in.

Though if she were this open, I'm surprised that she's not the killer... then again, she wasn't murdering people. That I know of. I'm seriously starting to doubt how well I did know her.

The deeper I went into this house of petty horrors, the more I was seriously starting to wonder what Erin might have been doing while my back was turned—with my wife. I had a brief worry about what

Erin may have done with Jeremy, but that didn't fit, even with what I saw of her behind the curtain. I do my best not to make snap judgments, but Erin's secret faith bothered me twofold. First, that her faith seemed directionless, unguided, and again, open to anything that could walk in. Second, that it was secret. I always thought that Erin had been a little strange, but we were friends. Friends didn't hide stuff like this. Did they?

I try to be open minded, just not so open minded that my brain falls out.

One of the forensics geeks came up to the two of us. "We have a problem."

Packard gave her a look. "Really? Couldn't tell. Could it be one of Tommy's friends scattered all over the lawn in pieces?"

At the geek's look of horror, I waved Packard's comment away. "What do you have?"

"The victim had a wrist watch with the day and time on it."

I nodded. It had been a gift to Erin from Mariel. "And?"

"According to the watch, it was broken at eight PM the day before yesterday. Over 36 hours ago."

I was about to ask why that was a problem, until I knew several good reasons why. It meant that Erin had gone from my house to hers and ran right into the killer.

It meant that hours after it was done with Carol Whelan, he had already moved on to his next victim, with no cool down time. This would have been worrisome with a normal killer, to heck with something supernatural.

And third, if the killer had already had Erin by the time Packard and I were at the Carol Whelen crime even, then who had Packard and I talked to on the phone several hours after?

"Is there any possibility that it was broken deliberately? That the killer changed the time on the watch when he was done?"

The geek frowned. "Not impossible. But right now, it's not a bad approximate time of death."

I made eye contact with Packard and jerked my head to one side. "Alex…"

"Right with you."

We went outside to the back yard—though given that it was solid concrete, perhaps it would have been more accurate to call it the back patio. It was still set up for a full outdoor spread with tables, a BBQ, but most importantly, no cops or Crime Scene Unit personnel.

"So, Tommy, how you doing?" Packard asked.

"You don't want to know."

"Here's a question: how did we talk to the dead girl two nights ago when she was already being tortured?"

"Assuming the killer didn't see too many murder mysteries and change the time on the watch."

Packard looked at me like I was an idiot. "Like the killer cares. He went from torturing one little girl to death for eight hours, then came over and started working on Erin, possibly for 36. Why does he care about narrowing the window by a few hours?"

"How about your phone?" I asked. "It records conversations, just like mine. She should still be there."

Packard frowned and pulled out his phone. He cycled through his recorded conversations until it got to the one with the right time stamp.

There was a click, and a lot of static.

My voice came through: "Kinda. Listen, Erin, how did you get to my house today?"

More static.

Me again: "How about the way out?"

Static.

Me: "There was a crime in the neighborhood."

Static

"A kid. Carol Whelan. Do you know the name? The family?"

Static again.

I winced at the thought of my son knowing this girl. "Not yet. They're on the list."

More static.

Me again: "No. If I have anything else, I'll call you."

Packard looked at the phone as though it were possessed...which it might have been. "What the Hell?"

Exactly, I thought. Apparently, the demon's ability to screw up records wasn't limited to digital photos.

Packard pointed the phone at me like a gun. "Okay, Tommy, this is getting weird. I heard that phone call. I *wrote up* that phone call. Now, it sounds like nothing's there.

"Seriously, what's happening? One victim is friends with your little boy, and the second is your wife's best friend. And these guys usually have a type. They usually don't jump from prepubescent girls to adults. So far, I see only two connections: the mode of murder and you. So you wanna give me any theories, Tom, before we turn this investigation into a list of people who may hate you and your family?"

I kept my face placid for a long moment. He was technically correct. Someone did hate me and mine. Except that it wasn't a person but a supernatural entity from Hell.

That should go over well.

"You've been my partner for years. Can you imagine anyone who hates me that much? Have we even arrested anyone who hated me that much?"

Packard frowned. "Hayes is the only one I can think of, and he was crazy. And he's dead. So it's hard to hold a postmortem grudge."

I almost laughed at just how close Packard was to the truth...and then it hit me. What if the killer had been using someone who knew me to kill? What better way to chose a host for his murder spree than someone who already hated me?

"Why not?" I asked. "Two times is enemy action, isn't it?"

Packard paused, uncertain what to do with this sudden shift in thought. "Three times, actually. Twice is supposed to be coincidence."

"Not a big believer in coincidence. You?"

Packard gave a flicker of a smile. "Not really." He frowned again and looked back at the house. "We went all over that house, right? There's nothing we could have missed, you think?"

"No. Again, there was no forced entry."

Packard nodded. "Exactly my point. Who does that? How does he get in? Anyone you remember with the ability to walk through walls?"

"Jesus," I suggested, which was true but a dodge.

After all, if a demon could flip cars at me without touching them, was using telekinesis to unlock a door that far out of line?

"There are a few ways he could have gotten in," I answered for real, ignoring the first thought that came to mind. Unless Packard was faced with the demon, I had trouble imagining how I could break the news to him. "Including charm. If not that, then a police costume?"

"Come on. We'll ask if anyone saw anything for the last two days."

I'll fast forward through the boring parts. We circled Erin's entire block, as well as the three across the street from her corner property, if only on the off chance that someone may have walked past and seen something. This would have been easier if one of the blocks didn't have an apartment building on it. Even though we sent out a small squad of uniformed officers to tackle the problem, it still took us hours. Again, video surveillance was a bust ... but if the demon who had possessed Hayes was behind this, then it might have been able to conceal itself from any local cameras in the neighborhood.

Unsurprisingly, a demon who passed unnoticed in a tight community like Glen Oaks to kill Carol Whelan also managed to pass through unnoticed in a regular Queens neighborhood.

The next few hours were an even bigger waste of time as we poured through files of all those people I busted who weren't in the Tommy Nolan fan club. Thankfully, my entire career came after the advent of computerization, so everyone I ever arrested were available at my fingertips...really slow fingertips, with RAM speed of about 1GB —assuming the demon hadn't changed that, too

"Could be worse," Packard assured me, "we could be using Apple IIs."

I informed him that I was not reassured.

"You know what I don't get?" Packard asked.

"I hope yours is shorter than mine. There are plenty of things I don't understand."

Packard gave a flicker of a smile under his graying mustache. "This guy kills Carol Whelan because she's your son's friend. Even leaves you the care package. He kills Erin because she's a friend of yours. Then he goes after you at Creedmoor after delivering her heart. Why? There's taunting and then there's taunting. I don't even think Jack the Ripper was this interested in connecting with the police."

I nodded. "Jack only wrote three different letters over three weeks. Not two packages in two days."

"So he must really like you. Or want you on a spit." He frowned, then leaned back in his chair, thinking.

"Aw crap."

Off of my expression, he said, "What if he knows you, and you don't know him?"

Technically true...more true than false, really. "How do you figure?"

"You're one of these guys who's out in public a lot. You not only do this, but you're active in your parish, charities, things like that?"

That was unsettling. I didn't like to discuss that sort of thing, since it sounded like boasting, even to me.

Packard continued, obviously reading my expression. "Honestly, I figured out what you did in your off hours after the first three months of meeting you. Especially when you were rarely available to catch a beer. That's before I knew you didn't drink."

For the record, I was not then and am not now against alcohol. I just didn't like the taste. "What's your point?"

Packard grabbed his phone, unlocked it, and turned it to face me. It was a photo of the closet in the Carol Whelan crime scene. "Patron Saint of Detectives? What if he's seen you at all of these places, and concludes that you're just some goody two shoes who needs to be taken apart? He'd be a total stranger."

I shrugged. "Maybe. But we have to follow what leads we have. It's not like we have a lot."

Packard grimaced. "You know what? Get out of here. Go be with your family. You're going to have a tough enough night as it is."

Chapter 15

BLOW BACK

I came home, braced for the worst.

I opened the door, and this time, Mariel was already waiting for me. Her brown eyes were tinged with red as she gently hugged me. I replied in kind.

"I heard."

"Erin?"

"Yes."

I held her tighter. That was a problem of living within the precinct. It was far too easy to hear everything on the local neighborhood network. For all I knew, Mariel had heard about Erin before I had.

"Listen, you might hear some things about Erin in the coming days, and—"

"The crystals or the sacrifices?"

I blinked and pulled back a little so I could look her in the eye. "What did you say?"

"What were you expecting me to hear about? Killing animals or her crystal collection?"

I furrowed my brown. "You knew?"

Mariel gave me a sad smile and a shrug. "I was hoping to surprise you with that after I finished with her. But it won't happen now."

Finished with her? "Could you explain?"

Mariel hugged me closer and gave a deep sigh. "Oh, I've been working on Erin for a while now. Think of her as a conversion project."

"Huh. She knew what you were doing? I'm surprised she hung around."

"It helped that she had her eye on me."

Blink. Blink. *Well, didn't see that coming. Maybe I should have.* I went through a check list of things that could have made that problematic, but Mariel would have mentioned if Erin had gotten handsy at some point...either that, or I would have come home one evening to find Erin with a flesh wound.

"There anything *else* I should know?" I asked dryly.

"No. I'm just wondering if I should have told you this earlier. We could have talked her into staying later."

I winced. Keeping Packard out of the loop as far as the demon was concerned was one thing. This? No.

"Look, Mariel, I think we should talk. Where's Jeremy?"

"Up in his room, doing his homework. Or sleeping. I can't tell. He alternates."

I narrowed my eyes. "What do you mean? He went in today, didn't he?"

"Of course. He's just not sure if he wants to cry or push through."

"Gotcha. Can we sit? Because there's something I have to tell you."

I sat her down at the dining room table. I told her about my conversation with Father Freeman at Creedmoor, though I left out a lot of the graphic details of Carol Whelan's death, since it would also spell out exactly what had happened with Erin. I then got to the part I thought she'd have the most problem with, since I had the most problem with it—that I may or may not be a saint in the making.

Mariel didn't interrupt at any point. I put in enough caveats and "on the other hand" statements to more than make up for it. I spent nearly twenty minutes explaining all of it and trying to explain away most of it.

At which point, Mariel put her hand on mine. She said, in a voice so matter-of-fact it was laughable, "I believe it."

I had to stop, and I tried to start again three times before I could get a word out. "You believe it? How can you? I'm not sure I believe it."

She shrugged and patted my hand. "Humility is good for you. You won't get a swell head. Drink?"

She stood up and wandered into the kitchen while I was still speechless. I leaned forward, looking into the kitchen. "Excuse me, you believe this? You did hear what Freeman suggested, didn't you? Me. Saintly. I mean, really."

Mariel wandered back, with two Snapple bottles, and placed one in front of me. She sat down, leaned back, twisted off the top and sipped. "Why not? Have you looked at the C.V.'s of some saints we have? If Saints Augustine and Ignatius can make it, anyone can."

"Yes, but—"

"Let me stop you," she said with a smile. "You realize that, as a family, we help with nearly every charity event the church gives, short of the arts and crafts group?"

I gave her a little smile. "I thought no one under the age of 65 was allowed in," I joked.

Mariel ignored the jibe at the legion of blue-hairs who ran that group. "And to top that off, you deal with the worst parts of the soup kitchen, the homeless shelter, praying in front of abortion clinics, then you go out and do your day job. And you don't let it effect you. You're not exactly my biggest candidate for burn out."

My knee-jerk reaction was to think that I was a cop. Breaking up fights in the homeless shelter was part of my job. And standing around the prayer group around clinics was just to prevent any of the usual suspects from harassing them or starting a fight. So, that meant it was also part of my job.

The only part that really stuck with me was that no, I hadn't let it get to me like other cops had. *Perhaps because I pray harder? I've heard dumber ideas.* "Here's the real problem, then. The killer? He's a demon, and he's out to get me."

Mariel blinked once, then put down the Snapple bottle. She

stared at the tea bottle for a long moment. "I guess I should have realized it was about you," she said softly. "Two victims, one that hurt Jeremy, one that hurt me. Both hurt you."

I was not certain how to react to her statement. "You skipped right over demon."

Mariel blinked slowly, twice, and broke away from looking into the tea. "Oh. Yeah. I didn't get a chance to tell you. I stopped by the parish after Jeremy went to school. I talked to Father Ryan about last night. His first thought was demonic infestation. He was happy to swing by and do a walk-through of the house, saying a lot of prayers. We probably shouldn't have any problems tonight, but we should definitely keep to saying prayers with Jeremy before bed."

My eyebrows shot up. "Wow. And I thought I had a busy day."

Mariel smiled. "Well, your station shootout must have been eventful," she said casually. "What was it all over? Some perp named Rene Ormeno, you said?

"Yup. But that won't be a problem again. He's been transferred to holding at Rikers. The only way he's getting out is when the Marshals come for him."

"Good. Then things should be quiet."

That was one of the reasons that I married Mariel, even though she knew she was going to be marrying a cop. Why? Because she didn't worry about what could happen, only what did happen. As long as I didn't get shot, she didn't worry about it.

Then she asked, "Is that where you lost your overcoat? Because you weren't wearing that one when you left this morning."

"Ah. Yes. Well, I didn't finish telling you about my visit to Richard at Creedmore."

Her calm melted away to anger when I brought out that the demon attacked me with dual scalpels. She was especially quiet when I told her about the flying car that the demon flung at me like a card cable.

"I think," she said when I finished, "I'm going to talk with Father Ryan about exorcisms. He may know a guy. He was confused that we had signs of an infestation in the house. He'll be happy to know it's not because we bought it from some cultist."

I chuckled. "Or that we were playing with some of Erin's toys."

She smiled sadly. "True. I'll miss Erin. Though I won't miss her being a little handsy at times."

I raised a brow. She said nothing and sipped from her tea.

Then the gunfire started.

Mariel and I both hit the floor. It took a moment to realize that was two guns, coming from outside, and not through the windows.

"They're blasting through the door," I said, staring out across the carpet, under my kitchen table. "And probably shooting up the security booth while they're at it. Do you have your—"

Mariel thrust her revolver in front of me. "Hold them off."

I nodded, knowing what she had in mind. In part because we knew each other well, but also because we had a plan.

Unfortunately, part of that plan involved me having my service weapon on me, which wouldn't have been an issue if it hadn't been for the shootout that morning and the mandatory IA investigation.

I took Mariel's revolver, and we both made it to our feet. I held the gun ready as she ran for the stairs. When she was up the stairs, I ran forward, for the front porch. It was enclosed, so it acted like a foyer. The bullets through the front door kept striking the outer wall of the living room.

The automatic gunfire ate through the door, carving out a hole where the lock was.

The gunfire at the door stopped, though there was still a continuous stream of gunfire outside, at the security office.

I heard a magazine hit the bricks outside, and I shot forward, heading for the door. As he reloaded, I stuck the revolver out the door, ramming it into the gunman's stomach, and pulled the trigger. I fired three times, punching a hole right through him.

The shooter groaned, and fell backwards. I was tempted to grab his weapon, but it was too risky to head outside and grab it. I had three bullets, and there was only one shooter left.

Then the back door smashed in.

Aw Crap.

I spun around, still in a crouch, and pushed forward, gun high. I darted through the living room, and stopped where the living room met the dining room. I leaned forward around the edge, gun ahead, and had a great view back to the rear door. The invader swept through the kitchen and was still turning when I fired three times into him—two in the chest, one in the stomach.

And nuts. I'm out. Our Father, who art in Heaven, hallowed be Thy Name. Thy Kingdom Come, Thy will be done—

The front door crashed open, and I whirled back towards the sound. Another gunman stepped into my line of sight but was about twenty feet away. There was no cover for me to roll to. I couldn't dive out of the way. If I rolled towards the wall that separated the living room and the porch...he could just shoot through the wall and riddle me with bullets. I was dead.

From a crouch, I leaped straight for the gunman. If I was going to die, I was going to die stopping this bastard from hurting my family.

I flew right for the gunman and crashed against him. My shoulder speared into the gunman, slamming him up against the front wall of the house. I shot my hand up for his face, driving my thumb under his nose, forcing his head back. It was a heavily tattooed Hispanic, ink covering his entire face.

MS-13 again, huh?

I reared back with the revolver and swung, cracking it against the side of his temple. The gunman's head snapped back, but he remained standing, so I backhanded him with the gun.

It took me a second to realize that I had basically flown across the room. Literally flown.

Must find a prayer for Saint Joseph Cupertino, patron saint of pilots.

Then I heard the worst sound anyone has ever heard right behind them, the sound of a pump action shotgun. *I should have figured. Two in the front, and two behind.*

Then the gun went off.

Chapter 16

NIGHT PREYERS

I was a little surprised that I was still alive. I turned around, and there was the expected gunman, only he was face down on the floor. Again, he wore MS-13 tattoos, only on his arms. There was a great bloody hole in his back.

On the stairs, above and behind him, was Mariel, holding the household shotgun.

I let out a breath I didn't know I was holding. "Hi, honey."

She racked the gun again and smiled. "Tell me again how we don't need the shotgun? Five guns in the house were enough?"

I smiled faintly. "Fine. Next year, I get you a machine gun. Upstairs? We'll call it in and hunker down, just in case there are more of them."

There weren't any more gunmen. They were probably running out of gunmen local to the area. We were 15-20 miles from midtown Manhattan, and it would be difficult for most gunmen to get automatic weapons out in plain sight on the subway. You've probably already concluded the motive behind the attack. Not only did I arrest Rene Ormeno, I was easily pinpointed as the man who had stopped the attempted breakout that morning. Ormeno was apparently more important to the organization than anyone considered—which might explain why he had smelled so bad, if my sniffer really is an evil detector—especially if they were willing to take on a police station in broad daylight, and a policeman in his home...I would have sooner expected an attack when I was out on the street, not in my community, complete with local security—even though they were hit hard as well.

Packard was one of the first guys on the scene who wasn't a patrolman, having sped all the way from the station. He stepped into my bedroom, where I was huddled with my wife and son, and said, "Geez, Tommy, what did you do, take out a private ad in the paper to be shot at?"

Mariel looked up from hugging me. "Alex, shut up for once."

"We're fine, Alex," I added.

"I figured that part when I saw the dead guys on the floor. Nice to see that you've got the MS-13 crowd in your fan club."

"Thanks." I rolled my eyes. "Any leads while we were busy being shot at?"

"Nope. Sorry. It's not like we can just Google this and have evidence come up."

Blink. "Why not?"

"What?"

"Jeremy, could you hand me my phone?" I asked him. The little guy darted over to the nightstand and grabbed it, slapping it into my hand. I turned on the WiFi on the phone and went into the search mechanism. I plugged in all of the various and sundry facts of the murder: dis-articulation, dismemberment, having the brain sucked out with a needle.

The result threw me, on more than one level. In part, because I had spent days protesting it and every form of it that ever existed.

The only thing out there that really involved cutting apart a human being piece by piece and then sucking the brains out of the skull with a needle was an actual medical procedure.

It's commonly known as partial-birth abortion.

"Alex, I think you should send this over to Holland and Father Freeman. This is going to get ugly."

* * *

DOCTOR SINEAD HOLLAND, Father Richard Freeman, Alexander Packard, and I were in the coroner's office bright and early the next day. The body of Erin Quintanilla was between us, cops on one side, medical professionals on the other, and the sheet-covered corpse in the middle. This time, we had passed four sickly-looking assistants outside.

This was the fourth day since I had first encountered the demon, and this was the first time I felt like we had a hope in Hell of solving this particular case, and finding this demon once and for all.

Then again, this was very much a matter of *"If the dog chases the bus, what does he do when he catches the bus."*

Packard and I ran the partial-birth abortion idea past Holland and Freeman.

Holland's eyebrows shot up, eyes widened and her mouth dropped. Freeman's head dropped, and he face-palmed and groaned. The two experts exchanged a look.

"How did we miss this?" Holland asked.

Freeman shrugged. "I have no idea."

I gave the priest a half-smile, a dark sense of humor coming over me. "Maybe the killer has the power to cloud men's minds."

Freeman gave me a look fit to kill. He knew I wasn't actually joking. *"Anyway,* superficially, the two methods of murder seem similar."

Packard said nothing, and the doctor looked at a tablet the whole time. I presumed that she was looking at Carol's file on her personal tablet—it's not like the city paid for upgrades or anything. She frowned at the tablet, concentrating on the details. I don't think she heard anything we were saying. "Yes, there are a lot of similarities. Even down to the medical expertise in the dis-artic-ulation."

"I can testify to the scalpel," I muttered.

"Medical professional with an expertise in partial-birth abortion?" Freeman mused. He leaned up against an antiseptic white wall.

He stroked his chin, pondering a profile. "Let's face it, even under the rubric of that particular profession, that's a very narrow skill set."

"He'd need access to both of the medical training and access to the equipment of an abortionist. It's not like you could attach a syringe needle to a vacuum cleaner and use it on someone's brains."

Freeman nodded. "But even among abortionists, there aren't too many who even perform partial-birth abortions. It's rare to have someone deal out that sort of thing."

Holland nodded. "Not many people make it a specialty. I don't even think they consider it a specialty."

"Remember George Tiller?" Freeman asked.

"Who?" Packard answered.

"Kansas abortionist," I answered. "I think he was one of the—what, six?" I asked Father Freeman, "Abortionists who have been murdered in the 45 years since *Roe v Wade*?"

Packard scoffed. "Please. I think there were more killed off on *Law & Order*."

"Probably," I answered, "but he seemed to specialize in, well, this," I said, waving at the sheet-covered autopsy table. "Kansas law prohibits late term abortion unless two doctors state that the child would die regardless—he 'consulted' someone without a medical license at least twenty times that we knew of. Let's just say that he didn't provide a face that the profession wanted on their ads. I don't think even they were fans of his. I don't think anyone shed a tear over him except for his family...if he had any."

"Don't forget Kermit Gosnell," Freeman answered.

Even Doctor Holland made a face as she looked at her tablet. "Ugh. Him. That's someone I would like to have on my table someday, preferably in this condition."

Packard and I looked at Holland like she had grown three heads. Neither of us had ever heard her say a cross word against anyone outside of the crimes committed on her table. She barely even said a cross word against the people who placed victims on her table.

"Really?" Packard asked.

She looked up from her tablet. "Of course. That man didn't run a practice; he ran a butcher shop. Women left his operating room with infections, mutilations, blood loss. They needed more medical attention after he was done with them than before. Imagine issuing a medical license to a street-corner drug dealer who owned a butcher shop, and you have the idea. I'd have added kidnapping, since he detained women who needed attention and tried to leave. Then add the children he murdered after they were born, alive and well and breathing on their own, a patient he killed through pure malpractice. Yeah, as a doctor, I didn't like him much."

Freeman raised a hand, just to get a word in. "Personally, if you want my opinion?"

"Yes?" Packard asked.

"You're looking for someone here who makes Tiller and Gosnell look like Mister Rodgers," Freeman said, looking from Packard to me. "Yes, I am saying this as part of a faith that looks at any abortion as a murder. But this is the difference between Jack the Ripper and the Holocaust. This will be someone other abortionists don't like. *They* might find him creepy."

I arched a brow at Freeman. He was giving me a profile like this was a person, even though he was the one who had suggested a demon.

Packard asked the actual question. "So what you're saying is it should be easy if we ask around a little?"

"No," Holland corrected. "It'll be easy if you can get someone to talk to you. Getting them to talk will be the hard part. The entire profession is used to being immune from investigation. There's a reason that cases like Gosnell aren't common—not because they're rare, but because they're rarely caught. An investigation here will be like pulling teeth. They'll think you're after them instead of one killer." She gave me a look with her smoky brown eyes. "How well known are you?"

I was taken aback. "What? I'm a cop, not a celebrity."

She rolled her eyes, and shook her head, exasperated. "I mean as a Catholic? We know it because it's you. Could someone find you on a

Google search?" She tapped the tablet a few times, tapped it again with finality, and waited. She frowned. "Uh oh."

"Uh oh? What uh oh?"

"You don't read the papers, do you?" she asked.

"No," I drawled, drawing out the word. "I'll look at the news on my phone, like most everyone else these days. I haven't looked at a newspaper since the *Daily News* cut out all the interesting comic strips...when I was fifteen."

Packard shrugged. "I have no time. And I get it all on my phone anyway."

"I do," Freeman says, "Why?"

Holland frowned. "I guess we're all out of touch these days then."

To be fair the time stamp on the story she showed us was after I left the station to come here. The headline was simple: CATHOLIC COP VERSUS SATANIC KILLER.

It was, of course, the *NY Post*, who brought you the classic headline *Headless Body in Topless Bar*.

And, even better, a photograph of me outside of my church was on one side, and images from the crime scene were on the other. They were several of the images from the wall of Carol Whelan's room, almost as though they had been taken straight from my phone.

It occurred to me that if demons could alter records in digital formats, what was to stop them from taking that data and send it to someone else?

Aw nuts.

"Thankfully," I said, "my phone has barely been able to function since this case started. So it's not like anyone can call me in to complain."

Then my phone rang. Holland looked at me like I had turned into a demon myself. "How did you do that? I don't even get reception in here." She raised the tablet. "This is on WiFi."

"Just lucky I guess," I answered. "Detective Nolan."

"This is the office of ADA William Carlton. ADA Carlton would like to see you and your partner within the hour."

I winced. *Of course the DA's office wanted to talk to me. Why not? Another time waster. Freaking demon, making me do more red tape.*

I made the arrangements with the DA's office to have a chat about the headline. Yay. I hung up and told everyone what the call was about.

Father Freeman sighed. "Good luck with that. Walk with me for a moment?"

Packard gave me a look, and I answered with a shrug. I followed the priest out the door and then followed him towards the washroom. Father Freeman looked around, making certain that none but the dead occupied the hallway. "I meant what I said," he began. "Even if I'm right about the demon—"

"Trust me, you are."

"Good to know. But the host for the demon is probably going to match similar to what I said. This host does this easily. He's along for the ride with the demon, and he doesn't seem to be objecting to murder. This guy? He liked the process of murder. He's had practice. Probably on low-risk victims: prostitutes, runaways, and perhaps even kids, and he may have graduated to killing adults to satisfy his urges even before he was possessed. And, frankly, the abortion aspect explains the Moloch angle, since sacrifices to Moloch included children. Demon or no demon."

"Right. The possessed aren't innocent bystanders. The possessed must have been into some serious crap before being possessed. Demons like to destroy souls. This one may have grabbed the first convenient psycho, and targeted you after meeting you in the station while he was in Hayes."

I nodded, and smiled. "At least, we're getting close."

Freeman nodded. "But keep in mind, the demon left you these images. He wanted you to know. He wants this."

I smirked. "But this time, I'm ready for him."

"Don't be too sure about that."

Chapter 17

POLITICS KILLS

Timelines are important in police work. Not only do we need to account for the movements of everyone around a victim and our suspects, we need to account for our own time as well. When we found what is as important to the case as chain of evidence and making certain we read Miranda rights.

Our timeline for that morning was relatively straightforward, since Packard and I knew what our day would look like ever since we forwarded our conclusions on the state of the victims to Father Freeman and Doctor Holland. Packard had picked me up from my house at 6:45 am, drove us to the station so we could clock in, then made it to the medical examiner's office by 9:00. The call from the DA's office came at 9:30, followed by a two-hour drive into Manhattan from the east end of Queens.

Since the address of the DA's office in Manhattan puts it near the southern end of the island, the neat and orderly grid system that is Manhattan's street layout falls apart, turning into a rabbit warren of streets that cross, merge, split, reform, deform, and generally melt down. In this case, the shortest distance between two points was a long and windy road of the Brooklyn-Queens Expressway, into Brooklyn and over the Williamsburg Bridge. Unlike the eternal gridlock that is Los Angeles, the drive wasn't a problem until the bottle-neck of exiting the bridge into Manhattan, at Delancey Street ... which merged into Kenmare Street. From there, we had to navigate the Lower East Side, through the Bowery and make a left down Centre Street ... and then a left on Worth and a left back onto Centre Street (Centre Street split around Thomas Paine Park), so we could get to 100 Centre street, where the Manhattan DA's office was at One Hogan Place.

If you ever wonder why it sometimes takes New Yorkers two hours to go less than twenty miles, now you know why.

On our way over (while we were parked on the Williamsburg), I wondered allowed, "Why does the Manhattan DA want to see us? It's not like we answer to him."

Packard had the seat back, eyes closed, while I drove. I had the patience for Manhattan driving. Packard had the ulcer. "It's the sensa-tional nature of the case. It already grabbed a headline, so expect him to muscle in. There's a good reason that Burkhead hates Manhattan, because Morgenstern treats everyone else like ambulance chasers. And he has major case in Manhattan, so expect that he will threaten to have the case jerked from us to give to them if we don't play nice enough."

That made sense. At least, if Queens DA Burkhead had wanted to see us, it would have been a nice, quiet 15 minute drive to see him in Kew Gardens. We could have even stopped at a literal cop shop down the street from the courthouse. Unlike *Law & Order*, which had had four District Attorneys over the show's twenty-year run, the Manhattan DA's office was more like a permanent position, and Morgenstern had been there longer than I had been alive.

But this is a reason that Packard and I worked so well together. Jesus said that we should be as innocent as doves but as wise as serpents, in part because evil will always be one step ahead of the children of light. Packard was the serpent.

We arrived at the office of Assistant District Attorney William Carlton and were told to wait outside. Both of us sat down and read through our notes on the case, making certain that we didn't need to consult them during the meeting.

My biggest problem with the case so far was not the murders, but how I'd screwed up. In order to save a few minutes, I had called Erin instead of visiting her directly. Had we done that, we would have made certain that she was alive and unharmed. Since the recording of our phone call with her had wiped her side of the conversation, we had no way of proving that we had talked to her or knowing that we had talked to her. For all I knew at that moment, the demon could have taken a break from torturing Erin to death in order to answer the phone, pretended to be Erin, and hung up with us to go back to work on her. I was certain that mistake would haunt me for as long as I lived. Could we have saved her? Or would we have left her, only so the killer would walk in after us? Or would we have walked in on a murder scene in progress, unwittingly facing a demon as it killed her and turned on us?

Yes, phrased like that, it made no sense for me to feel guilty, the odds of us stopping a demon in mid-murder was unlikely. But I'm Catholic. Guilt is a thing.

You might wonder if that was all I was guilty over. A demon had attacked my family, traumatized my son, and murdered a little girl because of a tangential relationship to me. If I believed a being that exists to pervert reality, it hadn't even been sent after me. It had recognized what I was, and came for me. It was like a bull sensing motion, or a hurricane touching shore. It was its nature.

I couldn't have stopped the demon coming for me. There was nothing I could have done to prevent it. Through no fault of my own, I was in direct conflict with a nightmare given form. There was nothing for me to feel guilty over.

But could I have saved Erin by taking a different course? I would never know while I was alive.

Noon rolled around before Carlton's office door opened, and the secretary brought us in. His office was bigger than a walk-in closet, but the space allotted for other people was limited. File cabinets had one wall, law books had the wall behind Carlton's desk, bookcases with loose papers had a third, and the fourth had an ottoman just wide enough for two underneath a window. There were two chairs in front of the desk, leaving it cramped for more than three people to be in the room at any one time.

William Carlton was a big man in several directions. He was 6'1", with wide shoulders, and a waistline that nearly matched but was just reigned in. His salt-and-pepper beard was a few days short of needing a trim, and his blue shirt and black tie were just neat enough. His suit jacket hung haphazardly on the back of his desk chair, and his slouch hat and great coat dangled perilously on the hat rack in the corner of the room.

He looked up. "Hello, gentlemen, please sit down. I hate to take up your time further, but there are things about your current case that must be addressed." He spoke in a deep voice that resonated with a measured tone, but his words spilled out in a sharp, clipped manner that spoke to a reasoned, thoughtful man but also a lawyer who was trained to appreciate Gilbert and Sullivan patter songs that were enunciated at a hundred miles an hour. I had hope he would be reasonable.

"While I normally wouldn't have brought you in, I am afraid that DA Morgenstern has some concerns about this Satanic killer."

My hope faded. Morgenstern and reasonable were two different lines of thought. "What do you need?" I asked, hoping that being straightforward would get us back to work faster.

Carlton smiled, not showing teeth, so we could only tell because the bush on his face moved a little. "Thank you for coming straight to the point. Right now, headlines are not what this case needs. If there are any leaks under your control, we would like you to plug them."

I shifted in my chair. "I'm sorry, did you just accuse us of tipping off the papers?"

Carlton's smile shifted a little but didn't fade. "No. You misunderstand me. If you find them, plug them if you can. Preferably, don't plug them with your bullets, though if you had to, I'm sure DA Morgenstern would understand. Probably. But now that we have headlines about two sensational murders, I'm afraid the clock has started on your investigation."

Packard scoffed. It was his *I saw this coming* noise. "Of course, it has. Are we allowed a full 48 hours from Erin Quintanilla's death, or do we have until eight tonight, counting from Carol Whelan's?"

Carlton nodded slowly, sadly, even. "You have until tomorrow. After that, it will be taken away from you. Are there no leads?" he asked hopefully.

Packard and I exchanged a look. Neither of us liked sharing theories and details of our cases with anyone if we could avoid it. Theories changed, stories shifted, witnesses lied. Constant updates would look like a series of dead ends as we tracked down every lead—because it would be. But right now, we only had one theory of the crime, and one connection between the victims.

Unfortunately, we had little choice in the matter.

"Right now, it seems to be a grudge."

Carlton nodded. "Against?"

"Against me."

We explained how Erin and Carol had been connected to me by my family. We also added that, since not even someone as cynical as Packard could find a criminal I had tangled with, the killer may have been some random psycho who had fixated on me, hated either cops, Catholics, or both, and decided to hurt me by attacking those close to my loved ones. The only detail I left out was that we could replace "random psycho" with "random demon," and everything else was relatively accurate. I chimed in with Freeman's insight that the symbols that appeared on the front page of the *Post* were indeed Satanic—or at the very least, demonic.

"Meaning that the headline was even more accurate than they realized," Carlton mused. "First time that's happened in my experience. But are you certain that this is some random nut job? Not someone you know?"

That's when we explained the method of the murder and what it pointed to: someone with proficiency in practicing partial-birth abortions and had performed so many of them. He had decided to move up in the world, to people who were already out of the womb.

"In fact, the symbols left behind fit in," I added. "Moloch was worshiped by throwing children into a fire pit. The Aztecs performed human sacrifice all the time. And the pyramid was something that Aleister Crowley used for his Satanic ensemble."

This was the point where Carlton settled back in his chair, and said nothing. His look became thoughtful, with pursed lips, hand on his chin, brow furrowed, as though he was doing mathematics. When he was done, he put both hands on the desk top, his fingers poised as though he were about to play the desk like a keyboard.

"One of the major concerns that you must understand is the massive undertaking you're about to go through."

Packard shrugged. "Gee, and I thought we were trying to prevent more undertakings, er, undertakers."

I tried to be more conciliatory. "Doctor Holland already informed us that we would be facing some intractability from the profession. Doctors closing ranks against outsiders."

"No, it's worse than that," Carlton advised, moving his hand along the edge of the desk. "The political power and influence of the abortion lobby in this city is ridiculous. Harvey Weinstein's sexhaustive victims proved you can get away with rape as long as you are pro-choice." Another hand movement, going the other way. "Every major politician in New York at the very least has to *say* that he's for abortion to one extent or another, because they control a large amount of currency, both political and financial."

As he talked, his hands moved as though he was working the scales or moving chess pieces. I realized that he *had* been doing math —political math, with equations and incantations so vague and amorphous, it made quantum mechanics look easy.

"You're talking about a group so powerful that they were caught breaking the law and nearly had the person who caught them prosecuted, while escaping themselves. In other parts of the country, they've had fetuses discarded as medical waste and sold to fire-burning power stations for a profit. This will be more difficult than you can comprehend. They have political friends. They have powerful wealthy friends, and they have lawyers. You must remember to tread carefully, lest you have the entirety of the ACLU breathing down your neck. Try getting a background check on an abortionist or investigate their clinics? It's a trial even for the health department to perform an inspection, because it would actually be racist."

I frowned, and my brow furrowed. "Why racist?"

Carlton looked at me kindly, like with an idiot child. "Where do you live in the city?"

"I don't live in the city," I answered. "I live in Queens."

"Ah. That would explain it. You live in the most diverse portion of the entire planet. One of the largest consumers of abortions in the United States just happens to be the African-American population." He cocked his head to one side. "May I ask where you are going to start your investigation? While their headquarters is on the isle of Manhattan, you have a stretch of them that goes down the length of the island of Long."

I smiled at his phrasing, and Packard answered. "We're gonna have to spiral out from our area. We're thinking that no one would come across the places he's famous unless he was in the neighborhood."

I didn't correct Packard on the killer's geographic profile, since I didn't have anything better to add. Especially since the host body for the demon presumably had a real life to get back to. That meant the demon needed to return him sooner or later. It was hard to explain being gone for a day and a half of torture and mutilation without a good reason. Going from Erin's kill site to the host's day job would make it someplace close by.

"Though to be honest," Packard added, "due to the internet, Tommy's admirer might be from literally anywhere."

"Including from Hell?" Carlton asked, amused. "Yes, I did hear about the message left for you by the killer at your station. It wasn't in the newspaper, though I'm a little surprised it wasn't."

"Will there be an investigation on where the information came from?" I asked.

Carlton nodded. "At every level. Including why no one at the paper contacted either of you, your Captain, or the Queens DA's office."

I crossed my legs, uncomfortable with the next thought that occurred to me. "Though I can't dismiss that they got their information from the perpetrator himself."

Both Packard and Carlton turned their attention to me. I shrugged. "We're not the only ones with the information. If he kept track of what he was doing as he did it, he'd know everything that we do."

Carlton leaned forward, looking at me closely, his fingertips on the desk as though he had paused in the middle of a concerto, and studied me as though I knew something I wasn't telling.

I gave him another casual shrug. "It's clear he wants to make it personal. I see no reason why he wouldn't try being thorough."

Carlton nodded slowly, considering and weighing my statement. I couldn't tell if he believed me or not, but he moved on. "First, I suggest you actually start your investigation up on Bleecker Street. The largest provider of abortions in the country have their executive offices there. Again, I ask you to be careful during your investigation."

"We're always careful," Packard answered. "It's in the job requirement."

"Yes. You take care around gang bangers and other criminals. What do you do among the professional classes?"

"Depends on the profession."

"How about businessmen?"

I laughed. "Then we're extra careful. Don't want to get between some people and money."

Carlton nodded. "Exactly. This is a billion-dollar business. Don't forget that."

Carlton leaned back in his chair and continued. "You're going to ask questions of a profession that is under intense scrutiny from certain groups. The paper headline led with your faith, Detective Nolan, so presume that they will believe you to be after all of them, not just a killer. After all, the Catholic Church states that their bread and butter is based on murder. Guess what all of them will naturally assume."

I flinched. Among the many reasons I keep my charitable activities to myself, that was an issue I didn't like dealing with. A healthy chunk of the population will hear *Catholic* and assume *Puritan*. Christ suggested praying in a closet in order to not put one's piety on display. In part, that was because the closet was usually the only way to get true privacy in a home 2,000 years ago. On the job, it was still good policy because more people assumed what my faith meant, rather than asking what it actually taught, or how I personally execute my faith. Saint Francis of Assisi found God in nature. Thomas Aquinas found it in reason. Father Vivaldi found it in music. Thomas More confounded all lawyer jokes. It was all part of the same faith.

Packard was the one who nodded. "Yeah. People get twitchy when we come around. Afraid we'll find all their dirty laundry."

"You assume they're hiding something?"

Packard actually smiled. "Everyone's hiding something. You're a lawyer. You should know that."

Chapter 18

DIGGING IN DARKNESS

I t took a while to find our way out of One Hogan Plaza and get to our car. By the time we were on our way, it was nearly one o'clock.

"What do you think of that little speech he gave us?" Packard asked.

Thinking was all I had been doing about it. We had been a little complacent in our own thinking. We had considered approaching the abortion community like we would doctors. I don't know about Packard, but I certainly hadn't considered that my faith would make our interviewees twitchy—but then, I had only had seconds before Carlton called us in. And if the abortionists were going to worry that we would or could discover any random secret or side line activity they might have going, this could get messy. In part because we bring out the best in people—their paranoia, their insecurities, and their suspicions. This was under *good* circumstances. When the ignorant believe that the Pope has put a fatwa out on them, it was easy to take the general paranoia and stack a few truck loads of additional suspicion on top of that.

"I think he didn't like giving us a deadline," I answered. "And he had some good advice. We're walking into a political mess, and he's a political animal. For a lawyer, he strikes me as one of the good ones. I even believe him that he didn't want to be horning in on the investigation like that."

Packard scoffed. I translated this one as *Yeah, you're probably right, but I don't want to admit it so I can say I told you so later on.*

"To Bleecker Street, as he suggested?" I asked.

"You're the one driving."

The Margaret Sanger Health Center looked as much related to health as your average bunker. It was a staple of early 20th century New York construction—ugly brown concrete, but at least the windows opened. There was a bright pink banner outside that read "Healthcare happens here."

I stared at the banner for a moment after I slid into park in front of a fire hydrant. "For a place whose main activity is killing children before they take their first breath, you'd think they'd realize the irony of that motto."

Packard chuckled. "Most people think irony is something that they take supplements for."

I sighed, and shrugged. I took our police placard and placed it on the dashboard. The last thing we needed was to be towed away.

I paused, with my hand on the placard. "Unless you want me to stay in the car. I would hate for you to take flak for me."

Packard laughed and rolled his eyes. "Please, Tommy, not a time for jokes."

I grinned and laughed. "Okay. If you say so."

We got out of the car. Two women were outside smoking. One of them said, "You can't park there."

I shrugged, deliberately revealing the badge on my belt. "So call a cop."

They sniffed at me as I laughed, moving past them. It was a little mean, but if you've ever met a cop, you'd note that our sense of humor is so dark, we make Hollywood's John McClane look bright and cheery.

I opened the door and gagged. The scent of evil wafting from the place hit me like a truck. It was worse than the MS-13 thug and as bad as the demon that had possessed Hayes. It was like someone had filled a morgue with the dead from two train crashes and turned up the heat.

I whirled away and tried not to heave my guts out. Packard stepped back, getting out of my way before I accidentally swatted him.

"What's the matter?" Packard asked. He took a step closer.

I straightened slowly. "The short version is that it I can smell whatever the hell they're working on in there. Call it a genetic quirk. Father Freeman explained it to me."

"Right. Yeah. Are *you* sure you don't want to wait in the car?"

I grimaced. Getting put down by simply the smell of evil wasn't going to be a good start. If I were close enough to God for him to grant me these gifts, then I had to stand up and roll with it. After the attack at Creedmoor, it was clear that I could at least get past the smell of evil from a demon at close range—especially if he was trying to carve me to pieces.

I said a quick prayer. "Let's go. If I hurl at any point, you'll know why."

Packard shrugged. "That happens, I'll just tell them you got sick from the baby parts in the cafeteria stew."

I rolled my eyes and clapped him on the back. "Thanks, buddy. I appreciate that."

"Anytime."

We went in, and identified ourselves at the front desk. "Hello. I'm Detective Packard, this is Detective Nolan. Could we by any chance talk to whoever's in charge?"

The man at the front desk sneered at us. "Do you have an appointment?" he asked in a voice so stereotypically homosexual, I suspected it was an act to fit in (Greenwich Village wasn't too far away). Of the gay people I'd met on the job, the few who were that overtly effeminate had been during the Village Halloween parade while I was walking a beat.

Packard leaned over with his badge, pressing it into the tip of the man's nose. "This is my appointment. Or would you like me to arrest you for obstruction, and see how you like prison shower rooms?"

The man's lower lip trembled. I sighed and rolled my eyes. Maybe he wasn't acting. "Seriously, dude? Man up. We want to talk with your boss. Just tell her we're here, and we're gone."

He buzzed us up.

As we went through the building, I found that the smell fluctuated as we went along. I didn't continually pray, but close. I paused every once in a while to track the scent. I couldn't tell if the scent of evil came from the abortions performed in the building, or the people who worked there. I had to hope that it was coming from the very act of abortions, instead of the people—then again, the law of averages would mean that I would catch the smell every once in a while on the street. Hopefully, that meant that these were good people doing bad things because they didn't know better.

My inner Packard told me not to place money on it.

The first time I actually noted a massive spike in the stench was as I walked into the office of the President, Joanna LaObliger. She was tall, bone-thin, Botoxed, and her hair was dyed purple. Her chin was strong enough to war with Bruce Campbell, and her nose long and sharp enough to replace the Wicked Witch in *The Wizard of Oz*. If I were casting her, I would have gotten Glenn Close or Cloris Leachman and tried to make her into a *Star Trek* alien, one of the ones Kirk jumped into bed with.

It didn't surprise me that LaObliger stank of evil. As Carlton had reminded us, this was a business. There were entire books discussing how many people in business could qualify as sociopaths. One of them was called simply *Snakes in Suits*.

"Hello, gentlemen, how can I help you?" she asked, not rising from her desk to greet us. I made certain to close the door and turned on the recording app on my phone. I had a very bad feeling that this was going to turn into a problem. And unlike patrol officers, we didn't get body cameras. I was suddenly regretting that decision.

I nodded, drawing her attention to me. I could trust Packard to get us past the front desk, not to be political. "Hello, President LaObliger, I was wondering if we could ask you some questions, using your knowledge of your professional community."

"Doctor LaObliger," she corrected me. "I am a medical professional and deserve to have the respect of having all my hard work acknowledged."

My eyes flicked to her right, to her I-love-me wall. "No, ma'am. Your highest degree is an MBA. I think President is already acknowledgment enough."

Her squinty eyes narrowed. "Did you just assume my gender?"

I didn't even blink. "No, President LaObliger. That would presume that I care what that is."

She crossed her arms and pouted like a child, probably because I wouldn't bow down to her authority. "What do you want?"

"We have reason to believe that there is a person within your profession that might be a killer."

"Aren't we all killers, according to your little *cult*?" she sneered.

Ah. She saw the newspaper. "A religion of one billion isn't really considered a cult," I corrected her. "In this case, we're looking for someone who would stand out among your colleagues. He might specialize in partial-birth abortions. He'd be considered strange by community standards. Does this sound familiar to you?"

LaObliger's face didn't change any. "You think one of our members is related to your satanic killer? Why? Run out of witches to burn?"

I kept my face straight as much as possible. Posturing like this was annoying, but not the first time someone we interrogated tried to cry victimhood. "Burning witches was mostly a Protestant thing. We were too busy with the Inquisition. At our crime scenes, the method of murder is distinctive, highly similar to a partial-birth abortion, including using suction on the brains through a needle penetrating the skull. So, again, do you have any colleagues who might match what I described?"

"I can't see any of our members like that. They're all perfectly normal."

Packard and I exchanged a glance. He shrugged. "That's an accomplishment. I've been a cop for thirty years. I don't think I've had a single normal colleague in that entire time."

LaObliger squinted at him. "You're cops. None of you are normal. You Catholics call *us* killers."

Packard scoffed. "Did I say I was Catholic?"

"The Vatican should look at how many people cops kill."

It was my turn to shrug. "Less than one percent of one percent of all law enforcement contact with the average citizen result in a use of force issue. You're fifteen times more likely to be killed in a car accident than even looked at by a police officer. Now, about the person we're looking for—"

"Not one of our people!" she suddenly barked. "Now get out!"

Packard and I didn't move, or say anything. After a moment, I said, "We're going to be asking questions throughout the various and sundry abortion clinics. If you could send out a company wide memo to help us out, that would be appreciated. Trust me when I say that you will not want this man running around your profession for any length of time. It will not end well."

"Really?" LaObliger drawled. "I guess you suspect that you're going to arrest any of us you think you can get away with. Are you going to have me dragged away?"

I pointed to the diplomas on the wall. "Obviously, you don't have the requisite expertise. And our killer is a rapist, so only your male employees might even be suspected."

"Unless you have some dangly bits you haven't had removed yet from a surgery," Packard quipped.

"Oh! Get out! Get out!"

As Packard closed the door behind us, Packard said, "So, what did you think of LaBitch?"

I smiled and held up a finger, holding him off. "Outside."

I left the recorder on until we got outside. Then I blatantly turned it off in front of him so he realized what I was doing. "I figure we need the cover. Politics."

Packard nodded. "So, LaBitch?"

"Paranoid. Obviously she thinks that we're out to get her. Can't tell if she actually has anything to hide."

Packard shrugged. "She could just be like that all the time."

I smiled. I wasn't that certain about it. Then again, I wasn't Packard. "How do you get to be this cynical?"

Packard gave a casual shrug. "I think it was about the time a girl discovered she was date raped only after the check bounced." He headed for the car. "So, was this a complete waste of time or only partial?"

"Not a complete waste. I suspect that this is a taste of what we're going to encounter."

I frowned as I opened the car. Now that I was out of the building, I felt exhausted. And dirty. "Ugh. Can we stop by a church?"

Packard gave me a look as he got in. He didn't reply until I sat, buckled up, and put the key in the ignition. Finally, he said, "Sure. I may even join you."

One of the nearest churches was Old Saint Patrick's, a church set in lower Manhattan that (obviously) predated the massive Gothic wonder that was Saint Patrick's Cathedral. On the outside, it was very "American Barn" architecture: straight walls up the side made up of gray stones, with a roof that was a simple obtuse angle. Inside, however, was an open-wide layout with Gothic pillars and arches that may have even inspired the one in midtown. It had only recently been upgraded to a basilica within the past decade.

I took a long moment to stand in the church, and soaked in the atmosphere. I took ten minutes to pray and another ten in the confessional—I had gone over the weekend.

Just as I finished my act of contrition, the bomb exploded.

Chapter 19

SUCH A MESS

Old Saint Patrick's shook. The windows rattled. The statues tottered perilously on their stands. Car alarms blared up and down the street, and probably further. If I weren't on my knees, I would have been knocked off of my feet.

I put my hands on my gun and twirled around. I saw Packard in the back of the church, grabbing a wall, and the priest opened his confessional door to see what had happened. Packard and I raced outside.

We were stopped by the still flaming wreckage that was our car.

Packard's jaw dropped, and mine was slack as well. After the fireball had settled down to a roaring campfire eight feet long, Packard looked at me. "This didn't use to happen before I was partnered with you. I have a long and distinguished career of being really boring."

I reset the flap on my holster. "What can I say? I'm popular."

Packard had his phone out already and dialing it in. As he tapped out the phone number, he asked, "You figure LaBitch didn't like our questions?"

"I wouldn't bet against it."

He gave a grim smile as he raised the phone to his ear. "Funny. I thought abortionists didn't usually set bombs."

I made my own call: to Mariel.

"Hey, honey," she nearly sang. "How are you?"

My eyes on the burning wreckage, I said, "Oh, you know, same old same old. Listen, you always told me how you didn't like the car they issued me, right?"

"Heavens, no. I swear it was like they wanted to kill your back. Why do you ask?"

"It won't be a problem any more. It blew up."

Mariel paused for a long moment. "Faulty fuel line?"

"If I had my guess? Bomb."

"Huh. It's obvious you weren't in it. What happened?"

I told her about the visit to LaBitch—dang it, now Packard had me doing it—and the subsequent stop at Old Saint Patrick's. There was silence at the other end of the line for a beat, and she said, "I concur with Alex. LaBitch suits her whiny little ass. Are you going to arrest her?"

"A little early to prove that."

"And, honey, you know what this means, don't you?"

I thought it over. That we were saved by a pit stop in the church was an interesting coincidence. Normally, I would have casually thanked God and moved on, thinking it a nice coincidence that God Himself had arranged. But after the way this week had been going, I was going to thank the Good Lord at length.

"Someone's watching out for me. I got it."

"I guess you'll be home late," she concluded. "The paperwork is going to be a bear and a half."

Mariel was right about that. If you can imagine the level of paperwork that the average detective had to fill out just for the day-to-day business of showing up and signing out, you can imagine the amount of red tape required for when the department-issued car explodes.

Despite all of that, we didn't find ourselves with a ride towards our station house, or even to the station of the local precinct, but to William Carlton's office once more.

"When I said that you should be careful, I didn't think you had the ability to provoke a terrorist act in the middle of the city," Carlton said calmly. "I ended up with a complaint from her right before I heard about your car problems."

My eyebrows went up at that. "Odd. Considering what happened with our car, I'm surprised that she issued a complaint at all."

Carlton smiled. "That presumes she's guilty of having your car detonated. But if she didn't call to complain, it would have looked even more suspicious—like she knew that you weren't going to be around to be yelled at. But when she called, she implied that you two were on a crusade to ruin her and her *healthcare specialists*."

Packard raised a finger. "Considering their business, I'd call them specialists. I think the mob does the same."

I recalled the way we entered her building and managed an appointment with LaObliger, then I played him the recording I made on my phone. He smiled, asked for a copy of the recording, and said, "This should at least keep her settled down. She probably felt comfortable making up details of your meeting, since you wouldn't be around to contest her side of events. I'll happily send her a copy, then imply that she's going to be hit with a subpoena for attempted murder—that should make some of her people very cooperative. And I'm going to have a conversation with your Captain to smooth over the car issue. I think you're going to have enough problems just talking with these folks without having to deal with transportation problems."

"There's also another possibility," I added. "It could be MS-13. I seem to have pissed them off. They could have planted the bomb. It's as likely as someone at LaObliger's office just *happened* to have a bomb lying around the office."

Carlton smiled. "Oh, I concur. But this is law, not justice, and the truth doesn't necessarily have anything to do with the legal system. Right now, innocent or not, I'm going to use this to leverage LaObliger to cooperate in your serial killer investigation...just curious, but you don't think *she* could have anything to do with that, do you?"

Packard laughed. "I can't see it. As I told her, she has the wrong equipment for rape, and as Tommy pointed out, nor the requisite medical expertise."

I shrugged. "It's not impossible. After all, look at the signs and symbols at the crime scenes. On the bodies. Counselor, if you walked in on that at a crime scene, what would you think?"

Carlton's look was curious, until it dawned on him. "That it would be a cult? And she could be part of it?"

I shrugged. "Anything's possible."

And it was. It had been over 24 hours since the demon attacked me at Creedmoor. Unless it had gone on to kill another victim, we had no idea where it had gone. We presume that it went on to the host's day job, before somebody missed the host body. That was an option, of course. The other options were that he had gone to LaObliger, the biggest name within the host's occupation, and talked her into joining it. Or, another option, there actually *was* a satanic cult in New York (where else would they go, really, aside from San Francisco?) run by LaObliger, and considering the MO the demon was using, why not?

"Another option is, of course, that we could leverage that against her. 'Hey, look, all these little demonic symbols line up with what you do for a living, and then you try to blow up the cops working the case. Maybe you're part of a cult that this killer is a part of.' "

Packard gawped at me. "That is sneaky and underhanded." He laughed and slapped me on the shoulder. "I didn't know you had it in you."

"I get cranky when people try to blow me up."

Packard was right. I generally didn't like playing games like this. But as I noted, it was still possible that she was involved with the demon. If she were, that would give her and her people ample reason to have an explosive ready to hand. Again, my money was still on MS-13, but perhaps leveraging LaBitch would be enough to catch this killer.

While it was tempting to push it further ... all I really wanted was to close the case. LaObliger wasn't the first whiny, backstabbing little cretin that I had ever met, so I had nothing personal against her. I had taken abuse outside of abortion clinics while the people I watched over prayed their hearts out. My issues with her were solely moral...

unless she did try to blow me up, in which case, I wanted her in jail. But the serial killer was more pressing. I still had no idea how to arrest a demon, or prosecute one. That was going to be a level of Hell all on its own.

Carlton lifted the phone, dialed out, and said simply, "Arrest her."

Packard and I exchanged a look. We didn't see it coming that Carlton had cops parked outside of LaObliger's office.

"Were you looking for an excuse to arrest her?" Packard asked.

Carlton smiled. "I met her at a fund raiser a few years ago."

Packard nodded. "Ah. Yes. I wanted to arrest her from the moment I met her as well."

I rolled my eyes, and we waited for the prisoner to be delivered to us.

LaObliger was dragged in, kicking and screaming a half an hour later. The way she struggled in the handcuffs defined "resisting arrest." Her purple hair was in disarray, and her arresting officers had to watch their knees.

Carlton rose to his full height, and bellowed, "SIT DOWN, YOU SQUABBLING CUR, AND BE SILENT."

Everyone was taken aback. The arresting officers took the opportunity to toss LaObliger in a chair and cuff her to the arms. She was locked in a position to face Carlton, and we were behind her, sitting on his ottoman.

"Thank you, officers," Carlton began. "Please wait outside in case we need you." He looked to LaObliger. "In case you have an interest in lying to me again, or lying to anyone else about what happens here, I will give you due notice that you are being recorded now, just as you were when Detectives Nolan and Packard visited you earlier. So your complaint there is hereby rejected."

LaObliger looked at us like she was surprised we were there in the first place. "I don't know who you think you are, but I'm—"

"*Be silent,* you foul woman, and listen. We have you connected as an accomplice to two murders within New York City, as well as the attempted murder of two NYPD officers. As the British say, would you like to help us with our inquires? Or would you like to be thrown into jail?"

LaObliger leaned forward and narrowed her eyes at him. "You want a lawsuit for wrongful arrest?"

Carlton smiled. "Really? Let's see how it goes during our deeper investigation into you, your finances, your company, and everyone who works for you. Yes, you may have politicians so scared of you that you've had every state regulation overruled and intimidated everyone into giving your rat traps a clean pass no matter its condition. Your doctors make the VA look impeccable; most of your employers could not even get past state licensure. Everyone with facts and evidence against you, you've tied up in court. But think very carefully about what a full-scale murder investigation would look like as the *police* storm your offices, your homes, your files and the butcher shops you call clinics. We'll see how you fare under scrutiny. I'm willing to play this game. Are you?"

LaObliger's squinty look didn't change. "You wouldn't dare. It would be racist. You'd be denying healthcare to every black in New York."

Carlton shrugged. "Depends on what we find. Federal Prosecutor Jackson is black and really wants to collect political scalps, left or right. So you tell me, LaObliger, are you certain that we can't find you and your people selling more baby parts or playing with finances? You got away with so much already. How much more do you think you can get away with before you become pure political poison?"

LaObliger winced. Doing the math on that was hard, even for me. Federal funding had been slashed, and they survived largely based on donations. If they were turned into a boogeyman by an actual government authority like the NY DA's office, she could kiss those goodbye, assuming he wasn't bluffing. And if she called him on it, even if he was serious, the prosecution would take forever and wouldn't help us any.

LaObliger finally sighed and sank bank into the chair, defeated. "What do you want?"

"Maybe this time," Packard snarked, "when we give you the profile, you take us seriously."

"What was it again?'

We sighed and ran through it again. She shrugged. "Well ... you know, we have one guy who's a little ... creepy, you might say."

"You sell baby body parts," Packard drawled. "So coming from you people, that's saying something."

She looked like she was going to gripe at Packard, then though better of it. "We occasionally have some think pieces in leading magazines, like *Slate*."

"Leading where? To the gutter?"

Carlton and I gave Packard the look. We had enough problem leveraging this out of LaObliger; we didn't need this derailed. He leaned back, and glowered.

LaObliger continued. "There was a *Slate* article a few years ago, March of 2012." Carlton and I brought out our cell phones and started tapping away at them, bringing up *Slate*, the year, and the topic.

The headline told me all I really needed to know about where it was going: "After Birth Abortion, the Pro-Choice Case for Infanticide," by a man named Saletan.

"He took it a little seriously," she said hesitantly.

I showed the headline to Packard, and his eyes widened. I held up my free hand to prevent his sarcasm from kicking in. I didn't react much to it because I grew up hearing about it from the bioethics chair of Princeton, as well as the man who had helped discover DNA. Yes, charming people.

"How so?" I asked calmly.

LaObliger shrugged. "You see, we don't *discuss* that a lot. Especially with outsiders. Sure, it would increase our bottom line, but the process of intact dilation and extraction isn't very common among our practitioners. We're just not *up* to child euthanasia yet. The country isn't yet at the point to have that conversation."

Packard looked at me like she was speaking in Klingon. I tapped out a note to him: *Partial-birth abortion is something even abortionists dislike doing, so AFTER-birth abortion isn't even on the table ... Yet.*

"Of course," Carlton consoled her, understanding and helpful, but giving me a look like *Humor the nutcase.*

"But Christopher Curran saw it and decided that it was the way to go," she said. "He's one of our more outspoken members on the topic. He's *the* premiere surgeon for intact dilation and extraction in the state."

Partial-birth specialist, I translated.

"How is he outspoken about—" Carlton coughed, "—child euthanasia?"

"He stated that it was clearly the next step of our healthcare services. An extension of the work that we're already doing." She shrugged. She casually added, as though she spoke about the weather, "He's right, of course, but we're just not *there* yet, you know."

I looked up from my phone and the notes I took, and Packard looked ready to leap out of his seat. Discussing the philosophy of a serial killer as being logically sound was like arguing that Hannibal Lecter's dinner menu was fine, but he just needed a better source of ingredients.

Carlton's expression didn't change at all, completely neutral and understanding. "Of course."

"Then again, Chris is really right about a lot of things," she continued. "When Pennsylvania and California filed lawsuits against those nuns to make them pay their fair share for contraception healthcare, he was one of the first people to send in his support letter. And when Doctor Gosnell was arrested, Chris knew *immediately* that it was pure racism. If Kermit had been white, it never would have gone to trial."

Carlton's smile became more of a rictus grin. She had already referred to one serial killer by his first name, and to ... whatever Gosnell was. I felt for him. "Where does this Chris Curran practice?"

She shrugged. "Oh, somewhere in the outer boroughs. Queens, I think. We can clear all of this up right now, though, I have his phone number in my phone—"

"No thanks, we'll contact him ourselves."

Chapter 20

CORNERED

Confronting a demon-possessed serial killer in the dead of night wasn't the way I wanted to go about it, but we had Christopher Curran as a suspect, and the sooner he was apprehended, the better.

We called from William Carlton's office to have unmarked cars stake out his house. I had argued against it. He wasn't onto us. Having officers there would merely tip our hand. The area was Jamaica Estates, a high-priced neighborhood where even our unmarked cars would stand out. I pulled out every excuse I could think of, and made up others, all to avoid the possibility of having dead cops on our hands.

Jamaica Estates was an upscale neighborhood. I wouldn't classify it as rich, but it was at least upper middle class. The demographics were small business owners and higher on the pay scale. The roads were well maintained, but it defined "if you don't know where we are, we don't want you," with winding narrow streets that ran wherever they wanted. While the perimeter was well defined, the roads within were anything but.

Packard and I had been given a new car. I didn't know where it came from, nor did I ask. I had also been given my gun back, since the investigation into the MS-13 shooting had been a formality, and it was clear I was going to be hip deep in a blood bath. By the time we made it out of the city and to Jamaica Estates, the sun had gone down, and storm clouds were already starting to gather for a nasty evening.

By the time we arrived, two blue and white patrol cars joined us, with no lights or sirens blaring. We were going to go in as quietly as possible.

We pulled up to the unmarked car, which was stationed a block down from the target house. We could barely see it in the dark. They had parked between two street lamps, so they were in a well of darkness between the lamps.

We approached them cautiously, since we didn't want to spook them any. We didn't need a blue-on-blue engagement. However, as we got closer, there was no movement. Neither of them had even turned to look at us in the mirror.

I rapped on the window. Nothing moved. I looked in the car, expecting to find two dead cops, there throats slashed from ear to ear.

The car was empty.

"There *any* chance they just went for a leak?" Packard whispered over the car.

I turned to the target house down the street, and put my hand on my gun. "Unlikely." I turned behind us to the patrolmen getting out of their cars. "Call it in. We have two officers missing from their station. After that, secure the rear. We're going through the front."

Three of them moved out while another stayed behind to call in from the car. He'd join the others when the call was done.

The five of us closed with the house, which was a one-story affair that was wider than it was tall. Packard and I went up the steps, and paused for a long beat before we knocked on the door.

Then the door swung open at the first knock.

We both drew our guns. "Never saw a time where that was a good thing," Packard said.

"Ditto." I told him. I didn't mention that as the door open, I was hit with the smell of evil. We were definitely in the right place.

I brought the gun up as I pushed the door open. The front hall was short, leading directly to a kitchen. It branched off to the right, into a living room. I took point, quickly sweeping into the living room.

Two men were nailed to the wall by their hands and feet, splayed open in an X. They had been stripped and fully castrated. With the pools of blood at their feet, I could only presume their cause of death had been exsanguination.

"Jesus," Packard whispered.

I held up a hand, signaling him to stop moving. There was another exit to the living room, to the left, around the large television. I pressed myself up against the wall until Packard tapped my arm. I wheeled around the entrance, into a dining room, nearly tripping over a chair. Packard was right behind me, over my shoulder.

Hail Mary, full of Grace—

Seated at the head of the short, rectangular table for 6, was a small man. He looked not much taller than 5'6"—five-eight at the most—and wore the same smug little smile he wore in the photo we had managed to find on Google. He was a middle-aged man whose light red (okay, a dark orange) hair was receding from the front, providing a widow's peak in front. His face was jowly and heavily lined. This was a man who had lived hard, played hard, and would never leave a good looking corpse.

This was Christopher Curran.

"Christopher Curran," Packard called, "both hands on the table. You are under arrest for the murders of—"

"Detectives Engel and Greaney," Curran told us. He already had one hand on the table. He flicked it towards us, flinging two badges onto the wooden surface. Both badges were covered in blood. "It's a pity you never knew them, Detective Packard. You would have liked them."

Packard circled right around the table, and I moved left. There was an opening into the kitchen on my side. "You have the right to remain silent, a-hole," Packard told him. "Use it. I'd hate for my finger to slip."

Curran looked at Packard and cocked his head like a curious dog at a new discovery. "Like it did in 1993?" he asked.

Packard stopped moving forward, startled. "What did you say?"

I looked at Packard in my peripheral vision as I realized something: one of the powers of a demon was to recite the sins of people nearby who had not gone to confession. I had the feeling that Packard hadn't gone to confession in a very long time. "Alex, don't listen to him."

The smell worsened as the monster continued. Curran didn't even give me a look. "You were a little drunk at the time, weren't you, Al? A New Year's Eve party at a friend's house. There was a robbery right in front of you. You shot him by accident. And it was an accident, wasn't it? Lucky for you, he had a gun. Your partner at the time swore he saw the robber turn towards you. But no one cared, did they, Al? But you did. You knew. And you said nothing. Then you lived the better part of the next year at the bottom of a bottle, didn't you? Your marriage was already on the rocks, and it tipped just that little bit further, didn't it?"

Curran leaned over just a bit further. "But at least your hand never left you, so something kept you company."

Packard stepped forward, pissed off. He stepped into the light from the kitchen. "Why you—"

I heard something shift to my left and remembered that this demon was telekinetic. "Alex, drop flat!"

Packard didn't even turn to look. He dropped down to the carpet without hesitation.

Knives flew right past me, driving into the wall of the living room up to the hilt. It must have emptied an entire butcher's block right at him.

I stepped forward. Curran shot forward from the chair like he had been standing, and he brought the chair with him, gripped in one hand. He slammed it against me as he slid across the table. He looked like a stunt man in a John Woo film as he bounced to his feet.

The chair hit me and drove me into the living room wall. I pushed off of it and flung myself backwards, heading for Curran.

—*pray for us sinners, now and at the hour of our*—

I was suddenly, miraculously, in front of Curran, blocking his exit to the hallway. I burst forward, driving my elbow into his face, then I hammered the butt of my gun against his head, leveling my gun at him. His head rocked back, and he staggered. He blinked, surprised. His nose bled a little, with a small rivulet of blood down his lip.

He looked at me and smiled. His brown eyes locked onto me. "Good," he said, drawing it out. His voice deepened as his pupils widened. "Very good."

"On your knees, you son of a bitch."

Curran said nothing, just wore the smile. His pupils kept widening, expanding until his iris was gone... and then kept expanding, swallowing even the whites of his eyes.

"Watch your language, boy," he hissed.

The television slammed into me, knocking me backwards, and ripping the gun from my hand.

Curran growled as he sprinted for the door. I grabbed the edges of the television and threw it at his exit. Curran slammed into it, tripping. I was on top of him in an instant, trying to secure him like I would any other perpetrator.

Curran pushed off the floor and slammed me into the ceiling. *Well, that's new.*

Curran spun us both around, clinging to the ceiling like Spider-man, and pushed off again, slamming me to the floor. I had enough warning this time to tuck my head so my skull wouldn't be split open. I felt something *crack* in my back, and it hurt so badly I could have screamed, but I wrapped my arms and legs around Curran and held on for dear life.

Packard came out of the dining room, gun at the ready. "Don't move, schmuck!"

Curran roared as he jump-kicked to his feet, with me still hanging onto him. He ducked one shoulder down, putting me in Packard's crosshairs, and bull-rushed him. Packard just barely stepped out of the way as Curran drove us both into the fireplace between the two murdered detectives. Curran crashed me into the drywall next to the fireplace, almost plowing me into a body. He elbowed me in the ribs so hard I felt them bend. I cuffed him on the side of the head with a closed fist, and held onto him with my legs as hard as I could, my back screaming in pain the whole way.

Packard closed, and slammed the barrel of his gun against Curran's head. He staggered a little but shook me like I was some bug that just wouldn't get off of him. He pushed at Packard with his foot. I wouldn't call it a kick, since it caused Packard to stagger back a few feet before falling over.

Then the dining room table shook. A chair nearly took Packard's head off as it shot for me. I shifted, putting Curran between me and the chair. It redirected in mid-air, slamming through the front window over the couch.

Curran spun around, putting my back to the dining room, and I knew what was coming. I dropped off of Curran and went flat on the floor, causing me to scream in pain. Two chairs went around Curran and embedded themselves into the wall, legs first. The next two went into the ceiling the same way.

I didn't see what happened with the last chair. I kicked out at the back of Curran's knees. The knees collapsed, and he fell forward, catching himself on the couch. I tried to scramble to my feet, but the shooting pain in my back stopped me. I flopped back down and reached into my pocket, grabbing my keychain—the small tactical baton.

As I flicked it open, Curran turned back to me, the black abyss of his eyes locking onto me like they were a void to suck in my soul. His hands came up, a scalpel in each of them.

"Time to die, saint."

Dear God, give me the strength to put this sucker down. I'm going to need all you can spare me.

A gun went off and part of the wall next to the body hanging there exploded in a puff of smoke as a bullet struck. Curran's head shot up, towards the dining room. I used the distraction to kick out again, driving my heel directly into his knee. He growled and fell back—apparently, even a demon couldn't make the host stand if the patella was out of place.

Packard fired again, clipping Curran in the shoulder. He looked at

Packard, snarled, and without any further ado, hopped over the couch and out the front window. Several gunshots went off and were silenced.

I held in my scream as I worked myself onto my stomach, then scrambled on my hands and knees to the couch. I looked out the window. On the front yard was one of the uniformed officers who had accompanied us here, the one who had stayed back to report the missing detectives from the surveillance car, was on his back, his throat cut open.

Curran was nowhere to be found.

I fell down on the couch, my back screaming in pain.

The back door was kicked in, and the other three patrolmen swarmed the place. Packard called out to them, "The suspect went out the front. He's on foot. Call it in."

"Ambulance," I croaked. The pain shot down my legs, as though it had only just started to *really* hurt now that the fun was over. I didn't want to imagine what it felt like after the endorphins and adrenaline wore off.

"That, too. Now go. Go. Go."

The three left to sweep over the rest of the house, calling in on their radios. When they left, Packard said, "Tom?"

I groaned. I considered moving to face him, but I couldn't. "Yeah, Alex?"

"What the Hell was that?"

I sighed. There was really nothing else to say except the truth. "Would you believe it's a demon?"

Packard shrugged. "After the day I've had?"

Chapter 21

WHAT LIES BENEATH

The paramedics who answered the call took one look at me and decided that the fight with Curran had shifted one of the discs in my spine. One of them set it with a loud *crack*, a move which also hurt like a bastard. They put me on a gurney, ready to cart me off, when I told them to leave me in the ambulance until we left—frankly, if there was an emergency, I'd tell them to leave me there and go. There was no paralysis but also no way of knowing what the diagnosis would be, so I needed to talk to Packard about our perpetrator before being carted away on a stretcher.

Packard only came into view the moment before he stepped into the truck. I was shirtless, and my body was a mass of bruises. He gave a low whistle. "Dang, man. You like you took the full brunt of a truck."

"You know, I had to keep him from breaking *you* over his knee, instead of me."

He sat next to me in the ambulance. "True. I have a low pain threshold for shattered rib cage. So better you than me." He glanced out the doors of the ambulance before he asked, "So, demon? Is there anything *else* I need to know that I can't learn from *The Exorcist*?"

"As long as you read the book, and don't go by the movie."

Packard nodded slowly. "And how did it know about me?"

"Demons know what sins you've committed that you haven't confessed yet."

Packard winced. "Anything else I should know?"

"I could give you a reading list, though you're better off with the nearest exorcist instead."

Packard looked like he was about to punch me in the arm, but he thought better of it. Those were bruised, too. "I'm better off with you and your superpowers."

My brow tightened. "Come again?"

"That's what she said," he snarked. "No, I mean one moment, you were on the floor of the dining room, the next you were in front of Curran. How did you pull that off?"

I winced. I hadn't given it any thought. It must have been bilocation—only it happened so fast, it looked like I had teleported. "There's the slight possibility that I might have been enabled with certain powers and abilities that have been associated with people who have later been canonized by the Catholic Church."

Packard gave me a flat, deadpan look. "You're a saint?"

"No. Saints are dead."

"So ... you're *going* to be a Saint?"

I rolled my eyes. "Not necessarily. It's complicated."

"So, where's the teleportation come in?"

I explained the concept of bi-location. "Enough about me. Curran—"

Packard held up a hand. "First, an APB was put out for Curran under a minute after uniforms broke in. I'm not sure what the heck we're going to do with him once we catch him. I'm afraid of what happens if we actually stopped him long enough to put the cuffs on."

I leaned back in the stretcher and closed my eyes. "We at least have him for assault and the deaths of three cops."

Packard frowned. "We have more than that."

I started. "What?"

"Remember the profile?"

I thought it over for a moment. Father Freeman had suggested that the perpetrator would have started from his day job, graduated to the high-risk population—either child runaways or fully-grown prostitutes. To my knowledge, there had been nothing in the daily reports about a serial killer running around. That meant the bodies hadn't been found.

I didn't need to guess at what was found inside the house.

I grimaced at the thought. "You found others."

"In the basement. Half of it is dug up, and buried. We're up to six so far, at various stages along the progression of his killing spree. Our official report is that he's just your average killer that worked his way up to full adults."

I groaned, partially in pain. "At least, we know who he is."

"Which we wouldn't if Curran hadn't gone after you. Or is it the demon that has a grudge?"

"The latter. The demon met me when it possessed Hayes at the station that morning."

Packard paused, then laughed. "That explains something at least. The profile was right, just some of the *how* differed." He looked me over. "So, can't you just do a miracle and heal up so we can can get back out there already? Heck, the teleportation thing is impressive enough. Just do it again, and project a healthy version of yourself?"

I gave him a tired laugh. "It doesn't quite work like that. I think. You're talking about magic. *That* tries to make nature and even God do what the magician wants." I'd have shrugged, but it would have hurt. "Mostly I hear about Saints healing other people. Not themselves." My eyes slowly closed on me as the day started to catch up to me. Usually, a day of driving in Manhattan traffic was enough to tire me out. Adding the fight was just the cherry on top.

My eyes then shot open. "Wait, you don't think I'm crazy. About any of it."

"Hey, I'm cynical, not blind. That thing threw chairs at us. And a television. It probably would have done the table, too, if we didn't drive him off." He gave a small smile. "And, dude, if you're not a saint, I don't believe anyone can be. Have you seen the kumbaya stuff you do versus the crap you deal with on a daily basis? I still do the job because I'd go nuts if I was forced to sit around all around all day doing nothing. You seem to like ... gah ... *helping* people."

I frowned. "What about your weekend parties? Your limbo competitions at the Caribbean day parades where you come in second?"

Packard rolled his eyes. "One, I can only deal with so many people so often and pretend to like them. Second, I would have *won* that limbo contest if it weren't for that woman from Hawaii."

My face bunched up as I thought back to the subject. "But you still believe my insanity. Seriously. Why is it that I'm the only person who has trouble believing that part?"

"Because," came a new voice. "Most saints don't believe it." Father Freeman rounded the opening of the ambulance doors and climbed in. He had traded his lab coat in for an overcoat. He sat near my feet and looked me over. "You've looked better."

"Thanks."

Packard gave him a poke. "Explain what you were talking about."

Freeman pushed his glasses up his nose as he laid back against the wall of the ambulance. "Saint Francis of Assisi put it best when he said that he was the worst sinner he knew, simply because he knew his own heart, and no one else's. That makes it difficult to consider oneself a saint in progress."

Packard sighed. "Got any thoughts on stopping this psycho?"

"My only real suggestion is don't kill him."

Both of us gave Freeman a look. "What?"

The priest shrugged. "Think about it. A bullet can't stop this thing. Putting a bullet in the head of Christopher Curran may only kill the host. It won't destroy the demon within. It would just cause him to jump to another body."

"Really? Are we thinking that we can just throw him into jail?"

Freeman shook his head as he pulled out a cigar. He didn't light it, just held it. "There should be an exorcism before he's let anywhere near the general population."

Packard smiled. "I don't know if it would be that bad. Lock the demon in with thugs? Lock them in and see what happens."

"I suggest you do, otherwise Rikers will become a bloodbath."

"Again, not seeing a problem."

I tuned them both out. Now that the perpetrator was identified, Curran had to be caught. The Demon had to be exorcised. "How about catching Curran?" I asked, breaking up their debate about the morality of turning Rikers into a massacre. "Do we need to do anything in particular?"

Freeman looked over the rim of his glasses. "You mean *Do I need to do anything in particular*, don't you? The entire NYPD is looking for him. I don't think you're Saint Christopher, finding the lost."

"I thought he was more GPS," Packard joked.

Freeman ignored him, and said, "There's no reason for you to be up and about, fighting the good fight, for what boils down to a manhunt."

"Though what will they do if they catch him?"

Freeman waved it away. "My point is that he killed three cops. Even the meter maids are hunting him. Even the Demon knows this. Unless it really wants Curran to be apprehended that quickly, it's going to keep its head down for a while."

I frowned. That was good, but this demon had made things personal since the moment I met him. This was a trail that led us straight to a monster, one that may not have even been caught had the demon not changed Curran's pattern. He had to have an endgame. He killed someone Jeremy loved. He killed someone Mariel loved. What was next? Someone I loved.

"Alex," I said, "you going to go home tonight?"

Packard scoffed, amused. "After the night we just had, I'm going back to the station. I may sleep there. Granted, given what we just saw, I'm sure that if this guy wanted to hit the 105th, it would look like the police station shootout in *The Terminator*, but it'll make me feel safer."

I nodded. With Packard off the chess board, that left one big target. "The patrol car is still on my house, right?"

Packard smiled. "Actually, there are two. Now that this guy is on the run, I wasn't going to take any chances. Especially when you consider that MS-13 still wants you dead."

"Really? You saw the way Curran flung that car at me in the Creedmoor parking lot. You think that two patrol cars are going to stop him? Heck, staying in the cars might even be too dangerous. You saw what Curran did to Engel and Greaney from the unmarked car."

Packard winced at the memory of the two dead detectives. "Still don't know how he got the drop on the both of them."

"Exactly my point." I nodded to them. "Could one of you guys call the house, see if we can get an update from them?"

Packard rolled his eyes. "I don't see why. He's on foot. Even if he wanted to, he couldn't be near your house by now."

I shook my head. "Pardon my paranoia. But my house is a casual walk of two hours from here. Ninety minutes for a fast pace and probably an hour at a run."

He scoffed, but pulled out his phone. "Fine, fine. I'll—"

His phone rang. He started, but answered it on speaker phone. "Yes? Packard here."

Jeremy's voice came through the phone, weak and scared, and sounding younger than he'd had in years. "Can Daddy come out to play?"

I jerked upright, adrenaline shooting through me. "Jeremy—" the sudden pain in my back stopped me.

In a smooth, slick, reptilian voice, the body of Christopher Curran spoke into the phone. "You have such a precious family, Saint. Don't you want to see them one last time?"

Packard's phone chimed. It was a text message telling Packard that Curran was in my house, and whatever Packard does, he shouldn't tell me.

Obviously, the demon had different ideas.

"Fuck you!" Mariel said. "Tommy, don't—"

She cut off.

"I look forward to seeing you, Saint." *Click.*

Packard and Freeman helped me out of the ambulance and into the police car. The first paramedic who tried to stop us saw reason when we told him what had happened and where we were going. The second paramedic wasn't as reasonable, and Father Freeman decked him. The first paramedic would explain the facts of life to his compatriot when he woke up. I wasn't too concerned, since I was split about whether or not I would be alive in the next hour.

Packard drove, lights and sirens blazing, and Freeman followed our trail. I lowered my aching body into the back seat, and held on along the way.

Dear God. Hi there. I hate to actually ask for a miracle, but I see little choice in the matter. A demon has my family. It is a demon that has done horrific tortures upon people I know and love, and total strangers to me. I do not know exactly what to ask for. If you could rip the demon out of Christopher Curran and cast it back to Hell, that seems like the easiest outcome. It would be most appreciated. If that's too much to ask, then I'm sorry. Perhaps I should ask for a temporary patch on my body, to make me able to at least confront this creature from Hell, if I must.

To be honest Lord, all I ask is for my family to be safe, no matter how You manage it.

Our Father, who art in Heaven...

Usually, it would take Packard twenty minutes to go from point A to point B, but we made it in ten.

It was already a nightmare. The street had been cordoned off by patrol cars. An Emergency Service Unit was down the street, securing the area, and a SWAT truck was already on site. Apparently, a cop's family taken hostage was a big deal.

It didn't help matters when I saw that there was a patrol car sticking out of my front window, with burn damage. The paint was scored and blackened, the tires melted and the metal twisted, and two charred skeletons in the front seat. It had been set on fire, but the flames had been quashed, even though I saw no flame damage on the house itself. The front door had been knocked off of its hinges and lay flat on the floor of the porch.

"I think you're going to need to find another place to live," Packard drawled.

I didn't even acknowledge the sarcasm. I reached for the car door and fought through the sharp pain in my spine. "Pull over. I'm going in."

Packard reached back and grabbed my arm. "You kidding? You're already beaten half to Hell. You want him to finish the job?"

"It ends here, Alex. It has to." I pulled my jacket on. The paramedics had sliced my shirt to pieces back at Curran's house.

Sgt. Mary Russell saw us and waved us inside the perimeter. The tall black desk sergeant had come out from behind her desk, just for me. "Good timing, guys." She held up her radio. "The psycho just demanded you come in."

Packard held up his hand. "Nah. He can't. Tell the psycho he's still a few miles out."

Russell shook her head. "No can do. He says he knows you're here, and you have five minutes to come in, or he ... hurts them."

"Call him back," I said, "and tell him I'm going to need more time, just to walk into the house."

It only took six minutes for the SWAT team to outfit me with a shirt, body armor, body camera, and another magazine for my sidearm.

I slowly creaked my way to the door. Muscle fatigue, my muscles, spine, arms and head all hurt. I felt as bad as John McClane looked at the end of a *Die Hard* film.

Our Father, who art in Heaven...

I had my gun in hand as I stepped into my house. I raised my weapon—slowly—before even stepping into the doorway to the living room.

There, in the middle of my living room, was Christopher Curran, his eyes both empty voids, as he held knives to the throats of both Mariel and Jeremy.

Chapter 22

DANCES WITH DEMONS

The demon possessing the serial killer Christopher Curran smiled at me as it held my wife and son hostage. Mariel's hands were locked onto Curran's arm, her feet dangling off the floor.

So much for that defense against a knife to the throat, I thought.

Despite knowing that I shouldn't kill this bastard, I had my front sight on his forehead. I didn't care about whether or not the demon jumped to another body, I wanted my family safe. It was already so blatant about its trail, I was certain I'd find it soon enough if I had to.

I met Mariel's eyes. "Hi, honey."

Curran smiled. "We're not that close."

"We're okay," Mariel whimpered. She looked unharmed, but her eyes were wide in terror, her hair looking like she'd been in a fight, and her t-shirt had been ripped at the shoulder.

"Daddy—" Jeremy started, until Curran jerked on him, pressing the flat of his knife into my son's throat.

"Now, now," Curran chided. "Mustn't distract from the real important part—me." He looked at me, the sick grin plastered on his face. "How did you like your little tour through the bowels of Chris Curran's employer?"

"I'm not a proctologist, thanks ... what do I call you?"

The head tilted to one side, as though it was considering my question. "Curran will do for now. The traditional names are just so cliché now."

Whatever the heck that means.

It continued. "Chris was the ideal host. He is just so *happy* working with me. I thought he was happy doing what he loved in his day job, but he's enjoyed me opening his mind."

I cocked the gun. I really wanted to blow his brains out. But that was probably something the demon wanted to happen—have Curran die, move on to another host, and start all over again. *Dang it.* "What the Hell do you want?"

Curran giggled hysterically. "Language."

"I was being literal."

Curran's eyes narrowed, trying to figure out if I was making fun of him or not. "I wanted you to learn *just* how much your life is an empty shell, as you serve a land that works for me and mine."

I frowned, and took my finger off the trigger guard. I kept an eye on his knives as they pressed against my family's necks. "Sorry. Not getting it."

Curran laughed now. "How stupid are you? You met President LaObliger. Have you not learned the depths to which your world will bow low to defend my lord? Haven't you seen the lengths to which your land will go to defend her and her ilk? Haven't you smelled the depth of the evil in their executive headquarters? They sell body parts and get away with it."

The demon must have seen something in my face, but gave a deeper laugh. "Yes. Yes. You see it. Where is your God now? Hm? My master *rules* all. *Consumes* all. *Everyone* you serve, serves my master. Even your *Mayor* would rather you and your brethren *die* than let a single criminal go to jail. How easy was it for me and mine to sic MS-13 on your police station? All over Rene Ormeno. Criminals that your city and your mayor would protect because criminals will vote for *them*." He jerked back on Mariel with his arm (not his knife). "Even Erin was a creature like my host. I could have possessed her at *any* time. She was so *open* to new experiences. She was so open to *me*." He leaned forward and stage-whispered in Mariel's ear. "Especially when I was done with her."

He gave me a look that made me want to kill him then and there. "You're alone. Your friends are weak. Your leadership works for me. And your God is willing to let them all live and go about *my* master's business."

I didn't have to think about it to know that the demon was right. Rene Ormeno and the MS-13 thugs that shot up my station and nearly killed my family had been kept within the United States because of sanctuary cities. Illegal immigrants like them were responsible for double-digit percentage crime across the country. President LaObliger and her minions were responsible for tens of millions of children killed inside the womb and across the country—the Holocaust had killed only a fraction of those that her company had--and sold the body parts.

But Hell, if the Devil could quote scripture, a little truth wouldn't be that hard to manage.

My arm was getting tired, and my patience was wearing out. "And you think...what? That any of that is *news* to me? That I stand guard over people praying in front of abortion clinics because I think nothing will *happen*? Are you a total moron?" I took a deep breath. Somehow, I was getting out of breath just holding my pistol. The aches and pains were starting to add up.

Then I smiled. "That was it? That was everything you did to destroy my faith? You *idiot*. My faith is in God. And your master may inherent this world, but mine is going to win in the end. That's why we pray together. As a family. Our Father, who art in Heaven, Hallowed be Thy Name."

Mariel and Jeremy took the hint, and continued with me. "Thy Kingdom come, Thy will be done, on Earth as—"

Curran's eyes bugged out, widening and lightening at the same time, as though the Lord's prayer had drained him. Jeremy's hand came out of his pocket with his rosary, and he flung it in Curran's face, making him flinch backwards. He dropped Mariel to her feet, no longer strong enough to hold her off the ground, but still maintained his grip around her upper body.

Mariel solved that with her elbow to his face. Her right hand still held onto his arm to keep from slicing her throat open. Curran's arm shot out, flinging her to the side. She was slammed against the wall.

This left Curran wide open for me to shoot him. I aimed for the right side of his chest, punching holes through his ribcage and probably his lung.

Curran looked down at his chest, confused. He looked up at me, uncomprehension in his eyes. "You didn't..."

With all of my strength, I burst forward, delivering a forward kick to his chest, like I was kicking a door open. This knocked Curran back, jarring one of the knives out of his hand.

The demon shook Curran's head, then roared and came at me.

I met him, throwing my right shoulder into the demon, my left arm coming up in a forearm block, the outside of my arm striking the wrist with the knife.

I stabbed the muzzle of the gun against Curran's elbow and fired. The knife dropped to the floor as the elbow exploded. Curran roared in pain; so his head was back, and his mouth was open when I elbowed him in the throat. He gagged and grabbed for his throat with his undamaged arm. I followed up by hammering him in the side of the head with the butt of my gun. I hammered through his head, opening up my hips, pivoting my entire upper body into the swing.

Curran fell back, dropping to the ground on hand and knees. He gasped in pain, keeping himself together.

Then Curran was a blur, pushing forward and coming straight for me... his first knife in his right hand. I brought my elbow tight against my body and tightened my right side. The knife drove in *under* my Kevlar vest. The blade came up like an uppercut along my ribcage, opening up my skin. I twisted to my right. The knife was caught between my vest and my ribs, so I jerked it out of Curran's hand.

Curran kept coming, driving me against the wall of my living room. He batted my gun hand away, then drove his fist into my face, then backhanded me.

My left hand came up under his wounded right arm and shoulder, up his back, and grabbed Curran's hair. I yanked down, pulling his head back. I jammed the muzzle of my gun into his shoulder and fired. Curran staggered back. He tottered for a bit, then his head shot up, locking onto me. He growled and bent his knees, ready to lunge again.

So I kneecapped him.

Curran cried out and collapsed to one knee. "This isn't over, Saint. I'll kill you, and your son—"

I kicked him in the face. He went down on his back, and he stayed there. I pulled out both handcuffs and my rosary. I Mirandized him as I proceeded to place the rosary around his neck, hopefully to keep his powers down while arrested. I cuffed him above the elbows, linking them by cuffing them together. When the demon was in Hayes, he had gotten loose by dislocating his thumbs.

Let's see him try it now.

"Dad!" Jeremy called.

I looked up from Curran to see my son with his hands on Mariel's neck.

Mariel was bleeding out all over the floor.

Chapter 23

WHAT DO YOU DO WITH A DRUNKEN DEMON?

I ran over to where Mariel lay dying. The knife had slashed at her throat as she was thrown aside. Her eyes were closed, and she was passed out. I grabbed her throat, and tried to hold her neck together with my hands. Blood welled up between my fingers, running over them and soaking into the carpet. Her long hair was covered with blood at the tips.

"Jeremy, run outside and tell the cops out there to send in paramedics!"

"Right, Dad."

I held on to Mariel's throat and knew that she was likely to die.

When the going gets tough, the tough start praying.

And I did. I threw all the basics in there. Then moved onto the Psalms.

Psalm 30: *I will exalt you, Lord, for you lifted me out of the depths and did not let my enemies gloat over me. Lord my God, I called to you for help, and you healed me. You, Lord, brought me up from the realm of the dead; you spared me from going down to the pit.*

Psalm 103: *Bless the LORD, O my soul, and all that is within me, bless his holy name! Bless the LORD, O my soul, and forget not all his benefits, who forgives all your iniquity, who heals all your diseases, who redeems your life from the pit, who crowns you with steadfast love and mercy, who satisfies you with good so that your youth is renewed like the eagle's.*

And for good measure, the popular psalm 107: *Give thanks to the Lord, for he is good; his love endures forever. Let the redeemed of the Lord tell their story—those he redeemed from the hand of the foe, those he gathered from the lands, from east and west, from north and south. Some wandered in desert wastelands, finding no way to a city where they could settle. They were hungry and thirsty, and their lives ebbed away. Then they cried out to the Lord in their trouble, and he delivered them from their distress.*

I kept going as my hands were awash in her blood.

I kept going when her breathing stopped.

I kept going even when the paramedics arrived.

I kept praying when I heard that she had lost too much blood.

I kept going when they tried to pull me off of her.

I kept going when they succeeded in pulling me off her.

· I kept going as they loaded Mariel up on the stretcher.

I only stopped when I heard a familiar female voice rasp, "Did Tommy get him?"

I whipped my head around to the paramedics. They stopped dead in their tracks, halfway towards the porch. One of them even had to quickly recover before dropping her.

Mariel's eyes were open. And she looked confused.

Thank you, God.

* * *

AFTER MARIEL HAD BEEN TAKEN out of the house, since the paramedics weren't going to take "miracle" as a diagnosis, it was back to the station for me. Packard had grabbed a sweater for me, an ugly thing that my mother had given me a few years ago that I barely brought out except when I went to see her. It was time for debriefing, interviews, and paperwork. This didn't even touch upon the insurance company paperwork that was in my future.

Given everything done to the body of Christopher Curran, I was once again visited by Internal Affairs. It was Statler and Waldorf again. I sat patiently in the interrogation room with the two older IA guys as they looked at the body camera video. Interrogation sounds ominous, but it wasn't—it was the only way to stop people from slapping me on the shoulders, which still hurt where Curran had rammed me into a wall earlier.

When the video was over, the IA men shrugged and even smiled at me.

Horowitz said, "Wow? You didn't kill him?

McNally nodded. "That's interesting."

Horowitz shook my hand, despite the dried blood. "Congratulations. We wouldn't have blamed you if you had gotten your wife and kid away from him, then shot him anyway."

"Good job," McNally concurred.

With a nod and another handshake from McNally, they left.

The next one after Statler and Waldorf was ADA William Carlton. He was more of a surprise. He walked into the interview room to join me. He lumbered in with a great slouch hat and a large black overcoat that ballooned around him. He carried a cane in one hand, and a briefcase in another.

He gave me a nod before settling in. "Detective."

"Counselor."

"Congratulations on apprehending Curran."

I leaned back in my chair, trying to relax. Now that everything had ended, I was starting to feel the pain again. I should have been surprised that I had held it together that long. Somehow, I had managed to get through the fight with Curran. I'm sure some people would have dismissed it as adrenaline.

"Thanks."

"I wouldn't relax just yet, young man."

"Hmm?"

"Is there something about the prisoner that we need to know about?"

"Such as?"

"Why he called you Saint, for one?" Carlton asked. "How he managed to hurl a police car through your front window, perhaps?"

"I'm surprised that no one else brought it up, either."

Carlton nodded. "I'm surprised about that as well. But I try to be observant. It's part of my job. The Creedmoor attack also had a car lying on its hood. And no one has asked about why chairs are embedded in the ceiling of the perpetrator's home. If I didn't know any better, I would ask what sort of super villain he was." He pinned me with a look as heavy as his voice. "*Do I know better?*"

I frowned, then looked around. "Is the camera off?"

"Of course. I don't want a record of this that I don't directly control."

I sighed. "In which case, you might want to bring Alex in. I can't imagine that you'll believe me unless I do."

"Please, Detective. We do not have two suspects together to coordinate their story. They—"

I interrupted. "Christopher Curran is possessed by a demon."

Carlton paused. His bushed eyebrows rose. He cocked his head to one side. "Let's bring in Detective Packard."

My partner joined us, and I began. I started with Hayes and explained the motive for its hatred, why it wanted to hurt me and mine, the attack at Creedmore, then Packard took over when we tried to arrest him. I didn't mention my abilities.

ADA Carlton absorbed all of this quietly, only interrupting to ask for clarification from time to time. His questions were slow and thoughtful, and usually in paragraph format. Otherwise, he took the occasional note on a legal pad, but that was it.

He looked at the two of us. "You do realize that none of this can come out during the duration of the trial. It would be a slam-dunk insanity defense for any lawyer. *The Devil made me do it* will almost certainly guarantee Mister Curran an extended stay in Creedmoor or Bellevue. Which, obviously, wouldn't help matters very much. If his employers pay for his lawyer—not out of the question, given LaObliger—then that will undoubtedly be the outcome.

"And I know what you're going to say. But nor can there be an exorcism before the trial. From what I'm aware of, they are trying on both the exorcist and the possessed. It would most certainly be considered cruel and unusual punishment and grounds of having the three of *us* thrown into prison right next to him, perhaps even automatic grounds for dismissal.

"On top of that, as I understand it, the possessed must *want* to be rid of the metaphysical parasite leeching off of their soul. I can think of no inducement we could make to Christopher Curran that would persuade him to have one. Being possessed gives a monster like him the powers and abilities equal to his own depravity. Honestly saying that he's a demon gives him a legal defense that would send him into an asylum. Making him submit to the exorcism willingly isn't something I think is possible.

"In short: there is probably no way we can fix the demon problem without causing us even more problems along the way."

I felt myself becoming twitchy as Carlton rattled off all the reasons that we couldn't do something here, and it really pissed me off, to be honest. "What do you think we're going to do with that guy if we drop him into the general population? Or do you really think that we can get away with calling for him to be in solitary confinement the entire time?"

Carlton shrugged, unhappy but helpless. "I can petition for it, but I can't imagine we'd get it. Happily, we're still finding bodies in his basement, so there is no way he can get bail. He will be in jail for the duration. I could make an argument that solitary would be for his own protection. He's a serial killer who targeted women and children, as well as a sex pervert. That is the perfect trifecta for being beaten to death in a prison laundry room. But if Curran, or the demon inside of him, states that he feels that he is under no such need of said protections, there's nothing we can do."

Carlton rose. "Right now, gentlemen, what we need to do is have him arraigned, prosecuted, and sentenced to prison for the rest of his life, and the next step after that can be finding out what to do with his demon."

* * *

THE DAYS that followed went downhill. Catching a serial killer possessed by a demon was the easy part, apparently. The real trial came for the detention and the prosecution.

When Christopher Curran was arraigned, the lack of bail was a no-brainer. Not even the Defense attorney argued against it, and he was a high-priced snake in a suit. But since Curran was wheeled in, the attorney argued that since the police shot Curran to pieces, it was only fair that Curran be treated by the state prisons. The next day, the newspapers of a certain bent decided that it was the tack to take— Curran had been shot in the joints, at point blank range, therefore the headline was easy.

CATHOLIC COP TORTURES ABORTIONIST.

Depending on which paper you read, the serial killer came into my home and threatened my family, so I *must have* tortured him ... or I found the next Kermit Gosnell, set him up for murder, and tortured him in my own home. They glossed over the five dead police officers killed trying to apprehend him. Further evidence of my insidious nature is that I coldly murdered several innocent Mexicans here on work visas when I didn't have to during an attack on the police station—a suspiciously vague recounting that didn't reference who attacked the station or why they did, only that I must have mowed down everyone regardless of everything except for skin color.

And people wondered why I didn't read the news. It was better for my blood pressure.

The "torture" narrative only lasted a week. Then Christopher Curran walked out of the prison hospital wing fully healed. Since it was impossible that a miracle happened and he was healed, the narrative completely went away.

Unfortunately, the trouble truly began at this point.

When Curran was in Rikers' hospital, three orderlies committed suicide. There had been no history of mental issues, personal problems, or that they had even been having a bad day up to that point.

They just killed themselves, all at the jail. The only commonality was that they had had contact with Curran.

Once Curran was let loose into the general population of the prison, two other inmates were killed within a matter of hours. They had been near Curran and had publicly threatened him.

It only took a whole day for the first riot to start. No one knew the cause, only that Curran was in the middle of everything and came out untouched.

Curran was then hurled into solitary confinement. That actually made things worse on the outside, but I don't want to get too far ahead of myself.

Personally, things kept coming at me. While the accusations of my torturing Curran were still actively in the press, I was suspended from the force. Given the condition of the house (there was still a car parked in my front window), we spent three days in a nearby hotel that was still within driving distance of Jeremy's school. (It was within walking distance, but that wasn't an option, given the past week). I made do with my suspension sleeping in and recovering from the beating I'd had in Curran's house. My back was healing slowly but surely.

Also, I spent plenty of time with Mariel. My wife had only suffered minor blood loss from having her throat slit. She spent the first week drinking plenty of fluids, and reading the nonfiction work *A Pius Man: A Holy Thriller*, a long winded account of the invasion of the Vatican a few years ago. It was only book one of three, that's how long winded it was. It had been written by someone else who claimed to be there. I believed him only because some of the descriptions were of the unreliably quality I had come to expect from eye witness accounts.

Once the accusations went away at the end of the first week, I was still kept off the job. Because no one wanted me anywhere near the streets until the trial was over. Which was stupid, but it was also political. Which is why you could call it paid leave.

Jeremy had been sent home from school at the start of the second week. Two kids had decided to pick on the "son of the evil cop" by cornering him in the school bathroom. Jeremy apparently grabbed one around the neck, like a hug, and hung on him, overbalancing him face first into the tiled wall. The next one was put off only slightly, but it was enough for Jeremy to flying knee him in the stomach and deliver a head butt that bled profusely. The bullies were both six inches and fifty pounds bigger than my son, which is why Jeremy was merely sent home, despite the damage he had left on them both.

When asked about being scared by the school, he denied it, saying, "A monster tried to kill me last week. They didn't scare me."

This led to an interesting discussion between me and Father Freeman with my pastor. It was a confidential talk that smoothed over most of the problems. Thankfully, Father Ryan was a priest who still believed in possession, otherwise I would have been worried the conversation would have ended up on the front page of a paper that already hated me.

By the time Curran had been thrown into solitary, my family had all moved back into the house. The car was gone; the window was covered over with plastic while the frame was rebuilt; the front door was replaced; and we could move in easily enough.

Unfortunately, that's when the protests started.

Once President LaObliger and her "people" had heard about Curran's confinement in solitary, she mobilized everyone on her Rolodex. He was a true champion and provider of women's rights!

Then the LGBTQMOUSE came into the act. Apparently, he was also a great supporter of "the cause," and a true defender of the right to love, no matter the age.

Not to be left out, the anti-cop BLM movement came out, and insisted that my wife was never assaulted, otherwise she would have been dead. Therefore, all of her blood found on the rug of my living room (which had been cut out and taken away by the forensics people) must have been planted. That, of course, *proved* that Curran had been set up.

All three groups tried to lead protests in front of my house ...

thankfully, they all got lost in the Glen Oaks neighborhood and were shown out for blocking traffic. They held a protest around my police station and, finally, around One Police Plaza—they could at least *find* One Police Plaza easily enough.

By the end of the second week, after even Internal Affairs told all three groups to go to Hell, someone fire-bombed my house.

Thankfully, whoever threw the Molotov cocktails were complete morons about it. Two came straight for my front window and my front door. However, the window was still covered by an industrial-strength sheet of plastic. The cocktails bounced off and onto the front lawn, where they burned the grass and scored the brick. The next two broke against my front door, which had been replaced with a metal door that only looked like wood. The brickwork on the stairs was blackened, and the new door became hot, and needed some paint; but, otherwise, nothing interesting had happened. Glen Oaks security responded to the fire by trying to run over the assailants.

Of the three groups, I had my suspicions, but no arrests were made.

At the start of the third week, Curran was let out of solitary confinement, since it was "torture," and the only way to shut up the rioters.

Packard called me in the middle of the night, at three in the morning, and I could actually hear him. My phone reception had come back after Curran had gone to jail...perhaps that was because most of the calls were to harass me.

"Tom, we have a problem. Curran has started another riot."

I paused, waiting for what this had to do with me. The prison authorities had quelled the last riot easily enough. I was on a month-long paid vacation that would have seen me out of town if I hadn't have obligations with the court and worried that Curran would have pulled something while I was away. "And?"

"It started six hours ago. They gassed the prisoners for hours, and nothing happened. They're thinking about sending in ESU and SWAT to put them down, but nothing's worked. They have all of the guards hostage. They're going to kill everybody if they're not released."

"Anyone in charge?" I asked. I didn't think that the demon within Curran would have been the public face of it, even if he had sparked it.

"It's Rene Ormeno."

Chapter 24

SPLITTING UP

Rikers Island tends to hold local offenders who are awaiting trial and have no bail, as well as awaiting transfer to another facility. Christopher Curran was awaiting trial. The transfer of Rene Ormeno was still pending, largely due to the mayor fighting the federal government over the meaning of "Asylum cities."

It can hold up to 15,000 prisoners. Estimates suggest that there were now only 14,000 prisoners, and falling.

On my drive over, it occurred to me that Curran hadn't caused a riot this massive and this problematic the first time was because he wanted me to endure more problems on the outside. Because why *not* cause more problems for me? It was what he had lived for, anyway.

I called Father Richard Freeman. He got through "What do you —" before I cut him off.

"This is Nolan. Listen, Richard, we've got a riot out on Rikers. I think you should call in an ecclesiastical SWAT team."

He hesitated for a moment. "Um, Tom? Do you think that we have Vatican Ninjas? Because, despite some thrillers, we don't have those."

"Actually, I meant start a phone chain where you call everyone you know to come meet me near Rikers and start praying. A lot."

"I'll see what I can do. I'm sure Ryan would come along."

There were several ways to Rikers, though it didn't matter, since most of the roads were still empty at that hour. Between getting dressed and getting to Rikers, it took a whole thirty minutes. I pulled out of Steinway, Astoria, and onto the Francis R. Buono Memorial Bridge, or Rikers Island Bridge to every sane person. It was a concrete and steel girder bridge that connected Rikers to Queens in New York City. It was the only path from Rikers, about 52-feet above the waters for vessels to pass underneath.

The bridge was already sealed off with ESU trucks mounted with machine guns parked at right angles to the side.

I got out of my car, and Packard met me on the bridge. We shook hands and strode towards the barricade. "So, what does it look like?"

"No idea how it started, really. The guards were taken hostage. They've seen enough bodies to estimate a thousand dead. And before you start thinking about priests to the rescue, the prison chaplains were all murdered. Except for the Muslim chaplain. He joined in on the mayhem and slaughter. We can't gas them and shooting them doesn't seem to work very well. Shooting them in the head at least puts them down, but that's about it. And let's face it, we don't have enough in the way of snipers to kill everybody. I don't think we have enough bullets if the entire prison just decides to rush us."

"Don't worry, I called in backup." I looked at my watch. "Give them about five minutes. Father Freeman is coming with my pastor and a few other priests from the parish. They're working on getting more."

"So, what do you think is going on? That Curran is somehow behind this?"

I sighed. I had thought long and hard about what was happening on the way over, and my conclusion was the worst-case scenario. But it was also based on something the demon said that I hadn't considered at the time.

I had asked the demon what I should call him. The response was simple: *"Curran will do for now. The traditional names are just so cliché."*

Out of all the demon names I could think of that had been made cliché, there was only one that came to mind. And when the demon used the plural, *names*, it made me even more certain.

"The demon lied. It is legion."

Packard stopped in his tracks and stared at me, his mouth ajar. He looked at me closely, like I had lost my mind. Then he closed his mouth and stayed silent for a long moment. His voice dropped, he leaned in to me, and harshly whispered, "Are you saying that we're dealing with hundreds if not *thousands* of inmates possessed by *demons*?"

I looked around to make sure no one could overhear, and said, "If you want to be picky, in the Bible, when Legion was cast out, he was driven into a herd of pigs. About two thousand of them."

Packard's mouth dropped open again. "Crap. We are so screwed. You and I could barely take *one* possessed psychopath, and now you're saying we may have two *thousand* of them? The entire NYPD, the gangs of New York and every redneck in the *country* couldn't physically subdue those guys. There's demonic infestation, but I didn't think they were like cockroaches."

I shook my head. "I don't think we have to directly engage all of them. At least, I hope not. I'm going to go in, and see if I can get to Curran again. If he's the source, maybe we can get the rest into him. Or if we can dispel him, maybe the rest will go. Either way, we have to try something. I'm not sure what happens if they all decide to rush the trucks. Because I don't think there is a good outcome to that."

Packard shook his head. "They may wait until they've killed all the non-possessed inmates, *then* rush us."

"Possible."

"My question is what happens first? How do we even get you across the bridge, man? You're suspended until Hell freezes over, and no one is going to be allowed on the other side of the ESU trucks until this is over. What are you going to do? Teleport again, like back at Curran's house?"

I groaned in frustration. "That wasn't teleportation, that was bi ... lo ...ca ... tion."

"Enough, Partner. I don't want to know that much about your alternative life style."

I ignored him. The light bulb had gone on. "Actually, Alex, that's not a bad idea." I frowned. "If only I knew how to trigger it on purpose. Maybe if I—"

I blinked and found myself on the other side of the prison gate, while still standing in front of Packard. I looked down the bridge at myself. I waved back at myself from the other side of the gate. I shrugged back. Prison-me ran for the front doors, which were already knocked off their hinges, the path strewn with bodies.

Packard's brow furrowed. "What?"

I smiled at him. "I guess it's working already. I'll call you when I'm ready."

He blinked and held his hands up to bid me to slow down. "What do you mean?"

Bridge-me smiled, walked around the back of one of the police vans, and stopped.

Then there was only me, running into Rikers island. I would have usually been worried about the various and sundry security doors, but the possessed inmates had been quite thorough in removing them from the hinges. There was blood everywhere, as though someone had tried to paint the walls in the style of Jackson Pollock. Inmates and guards alike were horribly mutilated and butchered. Several of them were missing at least one body part, and it took me only a moment to realize that these victims hadn't been cut to pieces but pulled apart. Probably two of the possessed had settled on a victim and played "Make a wish." At least one other person had had his head bashed in, possibly with the arm laying next to him.

That was less than fun.

The hallway reeked of carnage and blood, but above it all, the big, stand out smell of all, was the smell of evil. The smell of the demons.

Like a bloodhound, I was on it, shooting down the main hall, past all of the former security checkpoints, and over the bodies. I leaped over one patch of blood and landed in a slide. The blood was so slick it was like deliberately sliding on ice.

I stopped in the middle of two intersecting hallways and saw gangs ripping each other apart in each direction.

It occurred to me for a moment to just keep running forward in an attempt to hunt down Christopher Curran or even Rene Ormeno. They were all prisoners, and let's face it, decreasing the surplus prison population wouldn't be something that most civilians, or even police officers, would even care about. *Oh, look, we no longer have to feed thousands upon thousands of prisoners. Whatever shall we do with all of the surplus budget?*

Yes, I'll admit it freely, I have thoughts like that, too. I said I was a saint, I never said I lacked a pulse. After all, the faster I stopped the demons, the more people would stay alive. I was on a clock. I was busy. I couldn't be everywhere at once.

Then I stopped, smiled, and realized that I didn't have a concern about that.

Without thinking about it, I went straight ahead, saying the Our Father in my head.

I went left, saying the Hail Mary in my mind.

I went right, reciting the Glory Be.

Right-me led with a forward kick to the ribs of a bestial criminal with MS-13 tattoos. The foot planted in his ribs before I raked it down his leg, slamming down on the kneecap. It popped off of his leg and down his shin. He dropped in pain. Even someone possessed by a demon couldn't stand when there wasn't any support there, it was physically impossible. I whipped out my keys, extended the tactical baton, and slashed it behind the thug's ears, then backhanded it on the other side. When he didn't go down, I reached over his head, used his eyes for grips, and yanked back, exposing his throat. Instead of crushing his throat with my baton, I hammed down with my fist, making it difficult to breathe, but not lethal.

Left-me also led with a forward kick, only to a shorter inmate, so I clipped him in the back of the head, driving him right into a haymaker by an inmate. The possessed whirled around, saw me, and grinned horribly. The inmate behind him grabbed his head on both sides and threw him into a wall.

"Break the legs," I told him.

"Thanks, Detective," he said as he engaged.

I was taken aback as he stomped down on the knee, sideways, breaking it several different ways. He kicked the possessed one more time in the head, and paused, catching his breath.

It took me a moment before I realized that I knew this guy. He had been arrested for a bar fight where, to be honest, the other guy had it coming. He would probably be out in another month or two. He was also one of Daniel David "D" DiLeo's crew, and godfather to his daughter Julie. "Nate? Nate Brindle?"

He gave me a smile. "Yup. How you doing?"

"Not bad."

He nodded at the prisoner on the ground. "How'd you take that guy down? He ripped through at least six guys before you showed up."

"Healthy prayer life," I told him.

"I believe it."

The me that ran straight ahead just plowed in, slamming into a dogpile of orange jumpsuits, scattering several of them. There was a possessed on my right and my left. I hammered one in the face with my right fist, looked left and side kicked the other in the chest. I brought left foot down closer to that prisoner and delivered a side elbow into his face, rocking into it, putting all of my weight into a the sharp bone. That rocked his head back, making it perfect for me to hammer fist him in the head and spin into the right roundhouse that struck the rib so hard I know it bent. I grabbed him by the shoulders and drove my knee into him, leaning back into it, so my entire body weight was behind it. I hit him so hard, his feet came off the floor. I held my grip and spun, hurling him into the second of the possessed.

I had my baton out before either of them could recover, delivering an overhead blow to the first prisoner. I smacked into his collar bone, breaking it, and making the arm useless. I stabbed the point into his throat, distracting even someone possessed. The second one turned around as I was already whipping my baton into his face. That cracked a cheekbone, visibly dented his eye socket, and his head recoiled into the incoming punch of another inmate.

Breaking their legs weren't that hard after that.

Left-me asked Nate Brindle, "How's it looking?"

"Like a horror movie." He shook his head. "Worse. A nightmare. In a horror movie, you can at least slow down most monsters. I haven't seen anything stop these guys until you. What are they?"

Time for perfect honesty. I didn't have much for any other. Besides, Brindle had asked the right question, so he was already on the right track. "They're possessed."

He paused for only a second. "I was thinking zombies, but yeah, that'll do it, too. What do we do? Shoot them in the head?"

I shook mind. "Nah. They aren't the problem, the demon inside is. Kill the possessed, the demon might just shift hosts. They heal fast but breaking bones will stop them. For the most part. They're also telekinetic."

Brindle merely smirked. "That explains one or two things. How'd you drop him, though?"

"I was praying. That helps."

"Been a while since Sunday school, but I'll remember that. Now what?"

"I'm going in. The way is clear from here on out. You want to run, now's the time."

Brindle gave a feral grin. "And give up on a fight this big? Naw. I got friends in here need saving."

I shrugged. "Your choice. Remember, if you get anyone out, make sure your hands are up, and you listen carefully. Some of the possessed already tried making a break for it and got cut down. The rest of the department doesn't know what's going on in here, but they know these guys don't stop unless they're dead."

Brindle nodded. "Hands up; don't rush the cops. Got it."

There were gun shots from down the hallway. I whirled and grabbed for my gun. "Guards?"

Brindle shook his head. "These guys broke into the armory and have been passing out guns like party favors."

"Then they'll have to enjoy having someone shoot back." I patted him on the arm. "Let's go kick some ass."

Right me and straight ahead me had similar conversations with the other groups I had saved, and they took the opportunity to run the heck out of there. Brindle had barely asked me his first question when I had kept going in two other directions. I was hot on the smell of evil. One of me stayed with Brindle the entire way, and the other two tracked the scent.

And I began something I thought I had forgotten long ago, a prayer that I had looked up once on a lark, never thinking I would need it.

The rite of exorcism.

Chapter 25

RITE OF PASSAGE

To be perfectly fair with you, a priest is supposed to perform an exorcism. And a priest is supposed to get the permission of the possessed before starting one. *And the permission of the Bishop. And there were a dozen levels of bureaucracy and at least two dozen lab tests that needed to be done before approaching the Bishop*

And I was the one on the ground. With luck, I had a dozen Catholic priests on the outside praying their hearts out for me, and doing the same thing.

Lord, have mercy. Christ, have mercy. Lord, have mercy. Christ, graciously hear us. God, the Father in heaven, have mercy on us.

A scream welled up from the halls of the jail. It echoed up and down the empty cages of Rikers Island. It was a constant, kenning wail of rage and pain.

Straight ahead me launched a forward elbow into a possessed prisoner's face as he turned to face me. Teeth flew out of his head, and the darkness that were his eyes began to fade.

God, the Son, Redeemer of the world, have mercy on us. God, the Holy Spirit have mercy on us. Holy Trinity, one God, have mercy on us. Holy Mary, pray for us—

Right-me bowled over another group of the possessed, who were all writhing in pain, joining in the unholy baying, as though they were all about to be drawn down to Hell by the shadows that lay in the dark of the jail.

Left-me ran with Brindle, encountering a collection of ten gun-toting possessed who had been using the prisoners for target practice. One had grabbed a prisoner and hurled him into the air to be skeet when I had begun the prayer.

Holy Mother of God— I slammed the butt of my gun against the back of one head

Virgin of virgins— Brindle grabbed a riot gun and used it to choke a prisoner right off of his feet, then slammed him against the ground.

St. Michael— I hammered the one to my right with the gun, then kneecapped both men before I disarmed them. *Ora pro nobis.*

St. Gabriel—I shot a third one in the spine. *Ora pro nobis.*

St. Raphael—I stepped forward, grabbed the riot gun by the stock, yanked it straight up, and stomped on the man's knee before head-butting him in the face. *Ora pro nobis.*

All holy angels and archangels—Brindle clubbed a man in the ribs with the riot gun and swung it like a scythe into the face of the next man in line. *Ora pro nobis.*

All holy orders of blessed spirits—I head-butted a Russian gangster with a handgun. *Ora pro nobis.*

St. John the Baptist, St. Joseph—Brindle drove the shotgun down into a Blood's shoulder, dislocating it. *Ora pro nobis.*

All holy patriarchs and prophets— I kicked the last one in the knee while Brindle used the shotgun like a golf club and the man's head like the ball. *Ora pro nobis.*

"Nicely done," he told me.

I nodded. "Thanks, now we need—"

Then someone shot me.

As the other two of me ran, I recited the list of all of the saints I could think of.

Right-me slid across a hallway of blood, cutting the knees out from under a large Russian with a shank. He fell on his own knife. I came to my feet and kept running, annoyed that I couldn't have stopped that one from killing himself. But if the hallway of the dead I had just slid through were all his work, I wouldn't lose sleep over it.

I then had to stop as the flood of prisoners pushed past me, all of them trying to flee past the monster I had just put down.

At the end of the hallway, standing there calmly and serenely, while holding someone's head in one hand, and the body of a battered prisoner in the other, covered in blood, was Rene Ormeno. The blood had even obscured the bodily tattoos that had covered his arms. In fact, he had gotten new tattoos, this time covering his face, but instead of ink, they were made of blood.

With a final laugh, Ormeno smashed the prisoner's head in with the head he was holding, and tossed them both off to the side. Ormeno spread his blood-stained hands and grinned. "Hello, *pendejo*. Welcome to my escape. Do you like it?"

I didn't take my eyes off of him. "Too much red for me. Makes you look like a girl." *All holy apostles and evangelists, all holy disciples of the Lord, all holy Innocents—*

Ormeno didn't even react to the station, like I hadn't spoken at all. He reached into his pants and pulled out a shiv that looked more like a Bowie knife. "I made this 'specially for you, *gringo*."

Ora pro nobis.

I casually walked forward and spread my hands in a manner of a shrug. "I don't know. Seems like you're compensating for something."

Ormeno hadn't moved, and I considered just shooting him right there—one demon going into another body wouldn't be the problem that a thousand would. But this me had the tactical baton in hand and had been doing pretty well with it thus far. Giving away the advantage by throwing it at him or dropping it so I could grab my gun just seemed like a bad idea.

Also, there is something called the Tueller Drill test. The premise is simple: within 21 feet, a practice knife is drawn, and the assailant charges the one taking the drill. The average cop, gun in holster, has to draw down on the threat and stop it. Trust me when I say that the man with the knife had the advantage.

In this case, the man with the knife was possessed and could probably run faster than the average knifeman giving the drill. And I had blood all over me. If the gun or holster was just as covered, I was toast.

From all evil, deliver us, O Lord.

"Pity you had to have help straight from Hell in order to do it."

Ormeno charged. He was blindingly fast. The knife came up like an uppercut, ready to disembowel me. I barely blocked it with my forearm. I leaned forward so I could get distance from the knife and blocked almost like I was chopping down at his wrist. The strike lifted me off my feet, and I felt it up and down my arm. At the same time I delivered the block, I swung with my baton, catching Ormeno in the face. He growled and grabbed my wrist with his left hand. Without any effort, he flung me across the hall, into an open cell. The door had been ripped off of the hinges already, and there was no other way out.

Meanwhile, the me that had gone straight forward had come to prisoners' row, the main hall of cells, two stories high, with a wide catwalk as the only way to get around the upper cells. Easily two hundred prisoners could be caged there.

In all honesty, it looked like everybody who had stayed there was dead. Bodies and viscera all over the place. It looked worse than the sight that had greeted me at the main entrance to the Island. Some torsos had no limbs, and some were only partially pulled together. I didn't want to be the coroner who had to put this massive meat puzzle back together again.

But, easily a hundred feet away. standing in the center of the main floor, was Christopher Curran.

The serial killer wore an orange prison jumpsuit, and it was immaculate, completely unblemished and totally clean of blood.

From all sin, deliver us O Lord.

"Hello, having fun, are we?" Curran asked, smiling the calm, smug smile he had when I first clapped eyes on his face.

I carefully stepped over a body, never taking my eyes off of the smiling demon. "It's been a workout." *From the snares of the devil, deliver us O Lord.*

"Good. I'd hate to think I had made it too easy on you."

"Not quite. But it wasn't that much of a challenge. Otherwise, I never would have made it."

Curran shrugged. "We wanted to do this ourselves."

I cocked my head from one side, curious. "We? Which we? The Legion inside? Or you and Curran?" *From lightning and tempest, deliver us O Lord.*

The killer threw his head back and laughed, a sharp sound, as though razors could laugh. "Good. Good! I am *so* glad you figured that out."

I waved at the carnage around us. "It's hard to dismiss it when you're waving the evidence right in my face." *By the mystery of your holy incarnation, deliver us, O Lord.*

"True. But some men are dense."

On the day of judgment, deliver us, O Lord. "You seem to be in good shape."

The lights lit up with darkness, and he revealed his endless void. "You might have a legion of priests outside, and you may even be reciting the rite, but you cannot avail yourself against me, *saint!*" he spat the word. "I have dined on sin and suffering of more than any of my brothers in this body. I am the strongest of them. I have tasted of your fear and your pain, and the pain of *millions*. I walked the Earth when your great-*grandfather* had not even been considered a possibility by *his*. You cannot win. You cannot stop me. You cannot slow me. And this time, you're not going to get close enough to throw cheap rosaries at me."

Curran didn't blink or twitch his eyes, but the squelch of blood signaled me. I didn't know why I knelt and bowed my head, I just did. Someone's head flew past me. The blood from the hair rained down on me like a fine mist.

I heard another *squelch* and threw myself to one side as a boot nearly kicked me in the head. The severed leg shot past me like a spear.

I remembered back to my first encounter with Curran, with

Packard, in the killer's house, and remembered the chairs that threw themselves at us.

It occurred to me that the jail cell doors had all been ripped off of their hinges. So had the possessed ripped them off with their bare hands ... or had they even touched them.

The rip of metal to my right answered that question, as steel prison bars ripped out of their doors and shot at me like arrows.

During all this, left-me had been shot, and Brindle caught me before I fell. He returned fire with the shotgun, apparently just trying to keep someone's head down. Brindle pulled me off to one side as the prisoners being shot at by the men we had just felled all rushed out of the shooting gallery. They barely avoided crushing us but weren't so careful about the men who had shot at them for sport.

So much for not killing them, I thought.

"We have to get you to the infirmary," Brindle told me.

I looked at my arm, and blood was already running down it and dripping upon the floor. He was right. In fact, he didn't know how correct he was. It looked as though the bullet had nicked an artery. The brachial artery was one of those where a "nick" was lethal. It was like "nicking" the jugular or the carotid.

I grabbed my belt and pulled. "Tie this off, now. Or I'm dead."

We got the belt in place, but my guess was that I had easily lost 10% of my blood, and I was probably toast, even if I did get to the infirmary. If I was going to die in the line of duty, I would be happy with that. I just wanted to make sure that I did the job before I went.

"Not the infirmary," I realized. "The chapel. Where is it?"

Brindle shrugged. "Other side of the complex. Basically, if you had made a right instead of a left."

It was starting to occur to me why I had taken the third route. God had a plan, and He planned ahead. All I had to do was stay alive long enough for the plan to come together.

That you spare us, We beg you to hear us.

Unfortunately for me, I stumbled, fell, and let go of the belt.

I died shortly thereafter.

I was still also trapped in the cell with Ormeno on the outside, ready to gut me like a trout. His shiv was huge. But I had one advantage: it was pointed but not edged.

The MS-13 leader held the weapon in front of him. "My knife has not yet tasted your blood, *pendejo*. It is hungry for you."

I gasped as I pulled myself to my feet. "Where do you get these lines? Saturday morning cartoons or television *narcos*?"

He roared and came at me again, shiv held upside down like an ice pick, ready to drive it into my head.

I followed the first impulse that came to mind—I genuflected, my arms braced in front of me.

The shiv came in fast and hard—right into the wall. The shiv shattered as it hit the concrete, and my arms shot with the impact as he body-slammed me. I rocked back and pushed forward, trying to counter the force. It still felt like I had been slapped with sheet metal.

Ormeno reached down, grabbed me by my jacket, and hauled me up, off my feet. He shook me like a rag doll, then slammed me against the wall, roaring in anger. I felt bones break and shatter.

That you govern and preserve your holy Church, we beg you to hear us.

I had tucked my head, so I didn't crack my head open. And while he had me at a disadvantage, off the ground, he had forgotten one very simple thing: my legs.

I kneed Ormeno in the face. His head rocked back, his nose broken. He continued to shake me, but his grip wasn't as firm as he thought it was. I grabbed the hand on the right side of my body with both hands.

To be precise, I grabbed the thumb with both hands. And no matter how strong you are, one finger does not stand up to being pulled the wrong way by two hands and arms.

I broke the finger, and Ormeno blasphemed as he dropped me. I punched him in the throat. "That you humble the enemies of holy Church, we beg you to hear us." I boxed his ears in, and he flinched.

I roundhouse-kicked his knee. It buckled but didn't break, and he dropped, twisting around. I kicked him out of my way, made a left, past where I had first encountered him, and I saw the one door in the entire building that had been untouched.

Back in the main hall, I was busy being attacked. I rolled again this time to my feet, out of the way of the bars that flew like arrows. They stuck out of the floor like posts.

Unfortunately, they didn't stop coming. Metal ripped, tore, and shredded all over the place. I leaped again, but this time, one clipped me in the forehead, and a second ripped my coat. More came at me, fast and furious. One broke my arm, another the same shoulder.

The metal storm was unrelenting. Even when the bars weren't at the correct angle to stab me, they came at me from out of the walls or floors, wherever they had come in. The frames of the cell doors ripped and shredded and came at me next. I dove through the center of one, ducked and rolled under another, and a third clipped my broken arm, tearing a scream from my throat.

After only a few minutes, I was slowing down, the pain and the metal beating me down. In all that time, I had covered only half the distance between us. I was possibly only fifty feet away. And any time I tried a direct approach to him, it was too easy to predict, and metal came at me like a shrapnel bomb had gone off.

I won't say that it was a lucky shot that was my undoing, but my inability to think outside the box. I had been so focused on the shrapnel, I had forgotten the body parts. I had rolled to avoid a series of bars, only for a head to crash into my side. It stunned me for a moment, but that was more than enough

The first bar pinned my shoulder to the wall, tearing a scream from my throat.

The next bar pinned me as well, this time, punching a hole in my stomach and out my spine.

I barely even saw the others. They were one silver metallic blur as my eyes lost focus.

Curran finally took a step forward. He casually, calmly moved towards me, the better to see my agony. When he was within reach, I swiped at him. A bar shot out and rammed through my hand, pinning it to the wall. I must have looked like a caught butterfly on display with all of the various and sundry pins in me.

Curran giggled hysterically. "Uh uh uh uh. Naughty boy." He smoothed out his jump suit. "My mission is complete. Once I saw you, I knew that the plan I was summoned for could not go forward without ridding my master of you and your meddling."

I squeezed my eyes hard to get them to focus on Curran. But they wouldn't. "You were summoned? By a person?"

Curran merely smiled. "Yes. I was. I'd tell you the ingenious plan, but you're bleeding out too much. So sorry. Perhaps I should just put you out of your misery." Be paused, then laughed. "But nah, that would be just too *easy*." His eyes narrowed at me. The bars spun in mid-air, angled up at the catwalk above.

On the catwalk above, I was there, fresh from my fight with Ormeno, big black bag in my hand, and I threw it hurriedly as the bars came at me.

This time when I died, I barely even saw it coming.

On the floor below, still pinned to the wall, I saw myself with a bar going through my head like a bullet. My brains blew out the back of my head, and I watched myself die.

Curran turned to me and laughed. "So much for the rest of you. Given how easy you used bilocation, I was right to target you when I did. Any last words?"

I smiled at him. "God," I choked out, my own blood pouring out of my mouth, filling my lungs. "By your name save me, and by your might defend my cause...For haughty men have risen up against me, and fierce men seek my life; they set not God before their eyes."

Curran gave a condescending little smile. "You have that right, buddy."

My eyes darkened. *De profundis clamava te. Out of the depth I cry to you O Lord, Lord hear my voice.* "See? God is my helper... the Lord sustains my life...God... hear... my... prayer."

My head dropped, and I died, hanging on the chapel.

Curran gave a contented sigh, so relieved that he had seen the last of me and all of my doubles. He had seen me after I had split in the first corridor. Like my own bilocation, he and his demons were like a hive mind, all connected and communicating.

Curran turned, right into the syringe and I stabbed him in the neck and emptied the contents into his jugular.

The fourth me smiled into his face. After I had dealt with Ormeno, the one door that had been untouched in the entire prison had been the chapel. I had broken in and took all of the holy water they had in storage. I needed as much as I could. But that wasn't enough. I needed more hands. I needed just one more me. One that Curran didn't know about and couldn't see coming. He had destroyed me in the hall, twice, and once with Brindle.

The fourth me had been in the infirmary grabbing a needle. When I was killed on the catwalk, I had been taking the bag of holy water to myself. And I caught it.

And as I lay dying on the wall, pinned like a butterfly, I distracted Curran as I filled the large-bore, 85 ml syringe with holy water.

As I jammed the syringe into his neck, I said, "Holy Lord, almighty Father, who once and for all consigned that fallen and apostate tyrant to the flames of hell, who sent your only-begotten Son into the world to crush that roaring lion; hasten to our call for help and snatch from ruination and from the clutches of the noonday devil this human being made in your image and likeness." I grabbed him and shoved him up against a wall with all my might as I drove the holy water into him. "Strike *terror*, Lord, into the beast now laying waste your vineyard. Fill your servants with courage to fight manfully against that reprobate dragon, lest he despise those who put their trust in you. Let your mighty hand cast him out of Christopher Curran, so he may no longer hold captive this person whom it pleased you to make in your image, and to redeem through your Son; who lives and reigns with you, in the unity of the Holy Spirit, God, forever and ever."

I reared back, syringe half empty, and stabbed it into Curran's guts. As I emptied the rest, I looked at Curran's shocked, terrified, and wide eyes, I said, "The power of Christ compels you to go back to Hell and take all of your friends with you!"

Curran gasped and gagged, then he began to thrash. His violent seizures shook him as though the gates of Hell had opened up and reached forth to grab him and tear the rot out of him.

And then he screamed; a scream that came not only from his throat, but from two thousand throats from around the entire island. A scream of terror and horror that knew what fate awaited them back in Hell and back to their master.

Christopher Curran fell back against the wall, next to where I had died, and stayed there, stunned, as though he had been the one pinned there, even though nothing had been there.

He looked at me, eyes wide, and said, "You stole them from me. You *took* them from me! *YOU TOOK THEM FROM ME, YOU DIRTY FUCKING PIG! I'M GOING TO GUT YOU LIKE WE DID ALL OF THOSE GIRLS.*"

Apparently, Christopher Curran, serial killer, was alive and well and back in the land of the living.

Curran, the human being, grabbed one of the many prison bars that had been laying on the floor, picked it up like a baseball bat, and came at me.

After dealing with creatures that could move at preternatural speeds for the past month, Curran wasn't much to handle. I side-stepped to the right. He twisted to try and tag me but overcompensated. The bar went flying over my head, and his ankle twisted at an unnatural angle. He cried out in pain as his momentum carried him forward and past me. With the ankle sprained and his body twisted around, he lost his balance.

Neither one of us had noticed the true flaw in Curran's plan until it was far too late. I had been standing in front of several prison bars that the demon had ripped out from the cell doors and flung at me. They had embedded themselves in the concrete, and stayed upright at an angle, the jagged tears in the metal creating evil-looking sharp points straight up, like spears in a tiger trap.

Christopher Curran fell on his side, four bars punching through one side of his ribcage, and coming out the other end. He slapped at the floor, trying to shove off of the floor, as though pulling himself off the bars would save him. He thrashed and writhed, grunting and groaning. His eyes locked on me for a moment. They widened in terror and screamed, not at me, but where he was going.

He gave one more gasp, and went limp. His eyes were fixed and dilated.

Looking at him made me wince. "That had to hurt."

EPILOGUE

I walked outside of Rikers as the ESU and the SWAT team rolled in, along with what looked like half the cops in the city. I walked out without a spot of blood on me.

The first person to meet me was Nathan Brindle. He was cuffed but off to the side and seated up against a wall with a bunch of other prisoners who had just wanted to escape the massacre within. "How did you do that, dude? You died in my arms! Then you just sort of ... faded away. What are you? A Jedi or something?"

I smiled. The other bodies in the hall with Curran had also faded. It was disconcerting, and it had reminded me of the death of a Jedi. "You could say that."

"Yikes. Man, you have *gotta* teach me that Jedi mind trick."

"Deal. When I figure it out myself." I fist-bumped his shoulder. "You take care of yourself, man."

"You, too."

I turned away, and there was Packard, standing at the docks, hands in his pockets, calm and casual for all the world. He was smoking a cigarette, the first time I've ever seen him do that. I'd ask later and discover he bummed one off of a paramedic just before the floodgates of police opened up. "So, all done?"

I frowned. "Not sure."

Packard shrugged. "Whatever that means. Did you know you were on camera?"

I blinked, then looked at him. "They established a link with the Island security system?"

Packard nodded. "You should have seen them spin themselves into knots trying to rationalize you being in four different places at once. Their conclusion is that it was faulty time stamps."

I frowned. "But it was a live feed."

"Don't tell them that. It might break them." He nodded towards the dock. "By the way, you were right. The God squad showed up."

I looked down the bridge, and he was right. There, at the edge of the bridge, keeping clear of the opening so cops could pour through, were at least a hundred priests, in full cassock. They were all on their knees, hands clasped together in prayer, rocking back and forth like they were at the Wailing Wall. To this day, I don't know who had been the driving force behind stopping Curran and his demons, me on the inside or them on the outside. But at the end of the day, it didn't really matter, since the One who had done all the real work had been the One we all work for, and His son had been a Jewish Carpenter two thousand years ago.

I sighed. Either way, it wasn't my problem. My next problem was the reinstatement of my badge, moving to a new house, and most of all, Mariel and Jeremy. I'd have to call them.

"Thank God," I sighed. "For now. It's all over."

"What do you mean, *for now*?" Packard asked, suddenly suspicious.

I gave him my best consoling smile. I couldn't let go of the demon's final words to me. That it had been summoned. That it had been fulfilling a plan by whoever had done so. There was something else out there, something dark and twisted, and either stupid enough to use a demon, smart enough to control him, or evil enough that they and the demon were in perfect harmony, that the goals of one would fulfill the goals of the other. Whoever they were, I had wrecked their plans. I knew that they would probably be coming for me as well. Even my family, as the demon had.

I would explain to Packard of all the things Curran's demon had told me. Later. But the dark forces behind the demon were responsible for the deaths of friends, sleepless terror-filled nights for my family, and more pain than I thought I could ever live through... especially since I had died three times that night.

I was going to have to find them, and stop them.

I'd have said that God help whoever got in the way...but I couldn't say that. Because while I wasn't certain that I would ever become a Saint, or if I were a prophet, or an Agent of Heaven itself, I was certain of one thing at that time in my life.

I was on God's side. And He was on mine.

Which meant only Hell could help whoever got in our way.

Pro-tip: Never bet on Hell.

AFTERWORD

One thing that you'll notice I did not do was mention Planned Parenthood by name in this book, though I suppose that's implied by using the name and address of their executive offices in Manhattan. In the next novel, I will explicitly state that they are the Women's Health Corps. Wouldn't want there to be any confusion.

I cited a *Slate* headline, "After Birth Abortion, The Pro-Choice Case For Infanticide," by a William Saletan. It is a real headline, published March 12, 2012. Because I can't make this up.

I also make reference to "the bioethics chair of Princeton as well as the man who discovered DNA" being for infanticide. Look up the names Peter Singer and James D. Watson and come to your own conclusion. Though, truthfully, the man who REALLY discovered DNA was Gregor Mendel, the 19th century scientist and Augustinian friar who founded genetics—he just didn't have the name for it or the equipment to see it. James Watson would come along later, find the note in Mendel's notebook, and walk away with a Nobel for science.

Meanwhile, I should take the time to thank L. Jagi Lamplighter for the edits, Russell and Morgon Newquist for publishing the book you're now reading, as well as Margaret and Gail Konecsni of Just

Write Ink, and my wife Vanessa, for the beta reading and early draft edits.

ABOUT THE AUTHOR

Declan Finn lives in a part of New York City unreachable by bus or subway. Who's Who has no record of him, his family, or his education. He has been trained in hand to hand combat and weapons at the most elite schools in Long Island, and figured out nine ways to kill with a pen when he was only fifteen. He escaped a free man from Fordham University's PhD program, and has been on the run ever since. There was a brief incident where he was branded a terrorist, but only a court order can unseal those records, and really, why would you want to know?

He can be contacted at DeclanFinnInc@aol.com
    You can follow him on his Twitter and Facebook accounts: @declanfinnbooks
    You can read his personal blog at the following address: http://apiusmannovel.blogspot.com
    Listen to his podcast, The Catholic Geek, on Blog Talk Radio, Sunday evenings at 7:00 pm EST.

ALSO BY DECLAN FINN

SAINT TOMMY, NYPD

Hell Spawn

Death Cult (forthcoming)

Infernal Affairs (forthcoming)

LOVE AT FIRST BITE

Honor At Stake

Demons Are Forever

Live and Let Bite

Good to the Last Drop

THE PIUS TRILOGY

A Pius Man

A Pius Legacy

A Pius Stand

Pius Tales

Pius History

MORE URBAN FANTASY FROM SILVER EMPIRE

THE PRODIGAL SON by Russell Newquist

War Demons

Spirit Cooking (forthcoming)

LOVE AT FIRST BITE by Declan Finn

Honor At Stake

Demons Are Forever

Live and Let Bite

Good to the Last Drop

SAINT TOMMY, NYPD by Declan Finn

Hell Spawn

Death Cult (forthcoming)

Infernal Affairs (forthcoming)

PAXTON LOCKE by Daniel Humphreys

Fade

Night's Black Agents

CPSIA information can be obtained
at www.ICGtesting.com
Printed in the USA
BVHW071033121118
532888BV00012B/408/P

9 781949 891096